In Love with the
Wrong Side of the Law

Nikki Rae

In Love with the Wrong Side of the Law

Copyright © 2020 by Nikki Rae

Published by Tyanna Presents

www.tyannapresents1@gmail.com

This is a work of fiction. Any references or similarities to actual events, real people, living or dead, or to the real locals intended to give the novel a sense of reality. Any similarity in other names, characters, places, and incidents are entirely coincidental.

Synopsis

Thirty-three-year-old Andrea Moore, born and raised in Atlanta, Georgia, only had one dream, and one dream only. And that was to follow in her father's footsteps and become a Police Officer. After Andrea lost both her parents a couple of years apart, when she was just a young teenager, she was forced to move with her aunt on her father's side. Andrea's aunt made sure she did whatever she needed in order to graduate high school and pursue her dreams, which Andrea had accomplished. Andrea loved her job until she was put in a very compromising situation that she wouldn't have seen coming in a million years.

Javier Santos, born into the family drug business, became one of the largest kingpins in the world. Javier wasn't to be played with. He would kill you just for looking at him the wrong way. Javier was all about his money and respect, and if you played with either, you could kiss your life goodbye. One day, Mr. Santos has a run-in with Andrea Moore, becoming instantly attracted to her, and she oddly was attracted to him. Both of them tried their hardest to forget about one another, but they just couldn't seem to get each other off their minds.

Andrea knew they could never be since they worked for opposite sides of the law. But will her badge keep her on the right side of the law? Or, will her undeniable chemistry for Javier cause her to risk everything that she worked so hard for all in the name of love? Let's find out as we take a rollercoaster, drama-filled ride in *In Love with the Wrong Side of the Law...*

Chapter One

Javier

"Nigga, what the fuck did I tell you about being late with my money?!" I yelled, crashing the butt of my gun into Sean's scowl. Sean was one of my workers, and he used to be one of my best men, but lately, he'd been fucking up. I don't know why these niggas played with me because they know I don't have any sense and didn't care two fucks about killing a motherfucker. "Nigga, go get my fucking money, and the next time it's late, you can kiss your life goodbye," I told him before walking off.

On my way out, I sent my driver a text telling him to pull the car around back.

The name is Javier Santos, and I was probably one of the youngest and richest kingpins out there. I was only twenty-five with more money than I could ever spend in a lifetime. My dad, Franklin Santos, used to be the head nigga in charge, but he felt like it was time for me to take over the family business when I turned eighteen. I didn't think I was ready for that kind of responsibility, but I couldn't have been more wrong. I lived for this shit. I swear this shit ran through my blood.

My dad stepped down so he could spend more time with my mom and travel the world. He had a rule. He always said no man should be over forty and still be knee-deep in the drug game. My father says at that age, it's about family. I was nowhere near that age, nor did I have a family or plan to have one any time soon.

I wasn't beat for no bitches or settling down. Hell, if ever. I trusted no bitch, and I never let a woman get close to me. There wasn't one woman outside of my mom and my baby sister that knew where I laid my head. I was born and raised in Camden, NJ, but I've been living in my million-dollar home In Alpine, NJ for the past two years. My parents and my sister, Shyanne, had houses about twenty minutes away from where I lived, but my parent's did so much traveling that they hardly ever stayed home. I stayed home damn near every night. I had no problem taking a two-hour ride home every night. That's what I had drivers for. I owned a few closer houses, but I rarely stayed at any of my other properties.

My parents were Franklin and Shanice Santos. They'd been together since the eighth grade. My father was Hispanic, and my mother was African American. My dad didn't play about my mom.

It was just me and my sister, Shyanne. I was only two years older than Shyanne, but as close as we were, you would have thought we were twins.

The family business was passed on to my dad from his father. If I ever had any kids, I wasn't sure if I would want the cycle to break or not. I guess I'll cross that bridge when I get there.

I'd just pulled up to the new club that I opened last month. Club Indulge was going to make me a lot of money. It was packed every damn day of the week. I didn't open on Sunday's and Monday's. I was interviewing three women tonight because I needed to hire an accountant as soon as possible. This was a legit business, so I had to have someone to handle the money part. I came in a little earlier so I could do a background check, as well as check out their social media pages.

I wasn't the type of man that trusted any and everybody, so I needed to know who I was dealing with. I put the posting online a couple of months ago, and only three people responded. So I was about to see what they were about and check out their work history. After looking up everyone, they all seemed pretty okay, but it was one woman particular that stuck out. Not only did she seem qualified, but words couldn't even describe her beauty. Not to mention, she had a body to die for. But I knew I had to be professional. I looked up her Facebook and Instagram, and she didn't appear to have any kids, but as I strolled a little more, it looked like she had a boyfriend. Her name was Kamyra Wilson. After I was finished looking up everyone, I decided to check my emails since I had another hour to kill.

Chapter Two

Andrea

"Andrea, I need to see you in my office, please," my captain said.

I walked into the office and shut the door behind him before I took a seat. "Hey, Cap, wassup?"

"I just wanted to make sure that you had everything you needed for tonight. It's a pretty big night," my captain stated. "I just don't want you to fuck this up. Javier Santos is a very dangerous man, and one fuck up could end your life. Your goal is to get him to trust you enough to open up to you about his drug business. And no matter what, keep your head in the game, and don't lose focus. This is a job, so don't go falling in love, Andrea. You cannot be with him. I need hardcore evidence to be able to indict and convict this guy. We've been trying to get him for three years, and you know this is a personal matter for me as well."

"Look, Captain. I know how to do my job, and I also know I have to report once a week to let you know what's going on. The last thing you have to worry about is me falling in love. This is just a job. Nothing more, nothing less," I assured.

"Good. That's what I like to hear. Well, here you go. This is your new identity. From here on out, this is your name. You're now Kamyra Wilson. You will create a character for her, and you will do whatever you need to do to get him to open up to you about his job operation. You could be undercover for months. I chose you because I knew you could do it. Here's the address to your apartment. It's a good thing you are a really good accountant as well. I'm sure by now he's looked you up."

"A'ight, Captain. I have to go. If I'm going to make his head turn, I have to look the part, and that's going to take a little time. I don't want to rush my beauty," I told him before heading out the office.

My name is Andrea Moore, and I'm originally from Atlanta, Georgia, but I moved to Camden, NJ when I turned fifteen, years after my father was killed. Two years before my father died, my mom had passed from breast cancer. My father was a police officer for ten years, and he died in the line of duty. He loved being a police officer, and when he died, I had to move to Jersey with my aunt. My mom didn't have any family up here in the states, and I didn't want to move to the islands. My father was black, but my mom was Jamaican and Spanish. To make matters worse, I didn't know my mom's side of the family. But my aunt Tracy and my dad were close, so she's the one that took me in. My aunt Tracy treated me as her own, especially since she didn't have any children. I was an only child. I was told that my parents wanted more kids, but my mom was diagnosed with cancer not too long after she had me.

I'm a thirty-three-year-old police officer. Ever since I was a little girl, I wanted to follow in my father's footsteps. So as soon as I graduated high school, I did what I needed to do to become one. I loved my job, and going undercover was easy for me because I didn't have any family left, no kids, or a boyfriend.

My aunt Tracy died last year from natural causes. I had one best friend named Jessica, and I didn't have to worry about lying to her about being undercover. She was also a police officer at my precinct, so she already knew where I would be. Now I was going to have to get used to the new name and lifestyle. I'd been undercover before but never this deep. I wasn't sure how long I was going to be there because I didn't know much about my target's personal life. From what I'm told, he's never been seen with a woman and doesn't appear to have any kids.

It was almost time to go and meet Mr. Javier. I had to admit, he was kind of cute. I had to make him fall for me or trust me enough to talk about his drug business and money.

*****

I had a half-hour more of being Miss Andrea Moore before I became Kamyra White. It was the beginning of fall, so I decided on a burgundy pants suit with a white blouse and some heels. I threw on some light makeup and decided to wear my hair in a bun. Looking over myself in the mirror, I was happy with my appearance. I wasn't too much worried about getting the position because the two other women that were interviewing for the position were also cops. And they were to do everything not to get the job. I hoped in my Range Rover and peeled off. When I pulled up to the lounge, I hadn't even walked in the building and I was already impressed. Once I was parked, I took in my appearance once more and applied some lip gloss to my lips before strutting inside. When I walked in, the security asked for my name and ID, after giving him what he asked for, he let me in. I arrived ten minutes early with a folder, notebook, and pen in hand, ready to take notes. Although I was undercover, I still was hired for a job, so I needed to be prepared for it because I would be working as an accountant.

"Mr. Santos will see you now," a waitress walked over and said as she led me to an elevator.

We got on the elevator and stopped on the sixth floor. When we got off the elevator, the waitress walked me over to an office door. I was impressed with the décor of the building, and I could tell that Mr. Santos had exquisite taste. The door opened, and when I was greeted by Mr. Javier Santos, my breath was immediately caught in my throat. I knew that he was nice looking from the photos that were shown to me, and from the photos that I saw on his Facebook, but those pictures didn't do him any justice. But I knew I had to keep my composure and pretend that I wasn't impressed. I'm sure he was the type of man that could have anyone he wanted, *when* he wanted, and *how* he wanted.

"Hello, Ms. White. How are you doing on this lovely evening?" Mr. Santos asked, holding out his hand for me to shake.

"Hello, Mr. Santos. I'm doing well. How are you this evening?" I greeted, giving him my hand. Surprisingly, he kissed the back of it while looking me directly in my eyes. His stare was intense. I had to compose myself and be professional. "Do you kiss all of your interviewer's hands?

If so, I think it's highly unprofessional," I said to him seriously.

"My apologies, Ms. White. I didn't mean to offend you, but you're just so beautiful," he stated. "But you're right. That was out of line."

"Yes, it was, but I'm willing to forget about it if you are," I told him while taking my seat.

"I would appreciate that, Ms. White," he stated, taking a seat across from me.

I sat up and prepared for my interview. I wasn't worried about getting the position, but I was still interested in what he had to say and offer me besides himself.

"Your resume is beyond impressive, and I would love for you to work for me, but unfortunately, I can't hire you," he stated.

I unprofessionally dropped my mouth open, shocked that he said he couldn't hire me without even conducting an interview. "Mr. Santos, is this some kind of joke? You didn't even interview me."

"Ms. White, unfortunately, this is not a joke. I just don't feel like you're the right person for the job, but I can assure you that if I change my mind, I'll give you a call. Again, Ms. White, thank you for coming in," he stated before standing up and walking to the door.

I was so confused but didn't want to beg for the job and come off desperate. However, I needed to get in his life somehow. I knew when I called my boss, he was going to be pissed, but what could I do? I couldn't make him hire me. I got up and walked to the door.

"Good luck finding someone as good at their job as me," I said, walking off, making sure to add a little extra to my walk.

He mumbled something under his breath, but I couldn't make out what he said. I decided not to entertain it. As I was walking down the hall, I heard him call the next person in. When I got in the car, I called my best friend because I couldn't believe what just happened.

"So, when do you start and how was he? I want to know all the details," my best friend, Jessica, inquired excitedly.

"Calm down, Jessica. To answer your first question, I won't be starting. This nigga decided to not hire me without even interviewing me."

"What the hell do you mean he didn't interview you?"

I told her what happened from start to finish and she was just as confused as I was.

"Girl, do you think he made out that you were a cop?" she asked.

"I honestly don't know, Jessica. I told you everything that happened from start to finish. All I know is, Captain is going to be pissed. That's where I'm heading now."

"Yeah, that sounds crazy to me, but you know how theses niggas are. Call me back when you get finish talking to Captain. He about to lose his shit."

I just shook my head and ended the call because she was right about one thing. Captain was about to lose it. When I got to the station, he was on a call. Once he finished, I walked into his office, and he looked shocked to see me standing here.

"Andrea, what the hell are you doing here? What happened?"

I took a deep breath before responding. "He didn't hire me. He didn't even give me an interview."

"What the hell did you do? Do you think that he knew you were a cop?"

"I don't think so. I don't know what it was. He looked at my resume and told me how impressive it was but said he couldn't hire me. I was just as shocked as you are right now," I told him honestly. I told him everything that led up to that, and he just tapped his fingers on his desk.

"Something doesn't sound right, Andrea. Are you sure that you didn't say or do anything to raise his suspicion?"

"I'm sure that I didn't say or do anything at all. Maybe he just didn't want to hire me. My question is, what now? How the hell am I gonna get him to trust me, and I can't even be in the same room with him?"

"Look, we just have to come up with another plan. I'm sure there's another way. But for now, I still need you to stay at the apartment that I set up for you in case he changes his mind. Javier is a smart and ruthless man, so he's probably gonna check into you, even though he didn't hire you. Now that I think about it, him not hiring you was probably a power tactic. The only other thing I can come up with is he's extremely attracted to you and know if he's around you that he will go against his own rules."

Listening to the Captain talk had the wheels spinning in my head. Maybe he *was* trying to use a power tactic, or he could know that he wouldn't be able to control himself around me.

I sat and talked to the Captain a little longer before heading back out to the apartment. That would be my last time at the station until further instructed. The Captain didn't want to take any chances on me being followed.

The entire ride to my new home, all I could think about was Mr. Javier Santos. He was much finer than I thought he would be. In a way, I'm glad he didn't hire me because who knows how deep I would have gotten myself. I was already having a hard time not thinking about him now.

When I got in the house, I stripped out of my clothes, took a shower, and plopped down on the couch to find something on TV to watch. It was nights like this that I wished I had a man to come home to. I was single by choice because niggas was full of shit, and I refused to tolerate any nigga's bullshit. Not to mention the fact that my job was so damn time-consuming. I flipped on *Law and Order SVU* and watched it until it started watching me.

Chapter Three
Two Weeks Later

Javier

I'd just pulled up to my sister, Shyanne's, house. She called me to come handle some shit for her. I wasn't sure what it was because when she called, she said that she needed my help, and quickly, and to bring some strong men with me. I knew then that some shit popped off, but I knew I wouldn't find out what until I got there because we never spoke over the phone about anything. I parked around back, and when I walked in, my sister was sitting on the couch smoking a blunt.

"Wassup, sis? What's going on?" I asked. Shyanne held up her gun and pointed it upstairs. When I got to her room, it was two bodies in the bed. "Shyanne, what the fuck happened?"

"I came home on my break, and this nigga was in my fucking house fucking this bitch in my fucking bed, Javier!" she yelled. "And to make matters worse, this bitch is one of my clients, and she knew that was my man. So I killed both their dumb asses. He knows my ass is crazy, so

I don't know why he tried me. So, I need y'all to get rid of them for me."

I just shook my head because my sister didn't have any kind of sense. I sat next to her and ordered the guys to get rid of the bodies. They already knew what to do, so I didn't have to say much. Shyanne passed me the blunt, and I just took a puff before speaking. "Damn, sis. You put a bullet through both of their heads at one time. I guess all those shooting lessons paid off," I said while chuckling.

My sister was just as ruthless as I was. The only thing, she wasn't into the drug game. But she had the skills and could if she wanted to. Her passion growing up was doing hair and nails. So, she opened up her shop, yet she owned just as many guns and cars as I did. We both moved the same; she was just legit. However, I wanted a few legit businesses as well. That way, whenever I found my wife and had kids, I could offer them something other than the drug game. I knew that wouldn't be anytime soon because I wouldn't even let a bitch get that close to me.

"You fucking right. I walked in and heard moaning. I tiptoed upstairs and blew their fucking brains out. I bet they won't fuck in nobody else's bed," she said, puffing the blunt.

I just chuckled because my sister was hell. "I guess they won't be fucking again since you killed their asses."

I sat with Shyanne until her place looked the way it did before she killed two people. She ordered another bed and set it up.

On my way home, I couldn't help but think about Kamyra. I had thought about her for the past two weeks since the day she left my office. Baby girl was everything that you could ask for in a woman, which was the exact reason why I couldn't hire her. I knew she would be a major distraction, and I couldn't have that. She was already crowding space in my head that I wished wasn't the case.

When I got in the house, I had my maid, Claire, cook me up a steak dinner. I took a shower and smoked a blunt while I waited for the food to be ready. Ms. Claire and her sister, Ms. Diana, were two sisters that had been working in our family since before I was born. But since me and Shyanne were grown, and my parents did more traveling than anything. I decided to hire Ms. Claire to work for me since they didn't need two maids. Ms. Diana still worked for my parents, though.

Ms. Claire was like a mother to me, so she would always have a place with me until the day she left this earth.

I probably spent more time with her than I did with my own mother.

Ms. Claire buzzed my room to let me know that dinner was ready. I walked into the kitchen, grabbed my plate, and sat in the living room, which was something that I rarely did. I usually sat at ate at the table, but I decided to relax and put my feet up tonight.

*****

The next morning, the sound of my phone ringing woke me up from my sleep. I reached over and grabbed it. It was my right-hand man, Kye. Me and Kye have been friends since we were in diapers. Our parents were best friends, but our dads had been best friends since they were young kids as well.

"Yo', nigga, what's up? I'm about to slide through," Kye said into the phone as soon as I answered.

"Ain't shit up, nigga. Your punk ass just woke me up," I shot back.

"Nigga, tell Ms. Claire to whip us up some breakfast. A nigga hungry as shit right now."

I just shook my head and hung up the phone. I needed to piss and handle my hygiene. By the time I finished up in the bathroom, Kye's ass was standing in my bedroom.

"It's only nine o'clock in the morning, so you better have a good damn reason for waking me up and being in my damn house this early."

"Nah, not really. Besides, your house was closer to the chick house I just left. I met this bad ass stripper last night, and she doesn't live too far from you," he stated.

"Nigga, you slept at some random bitch's house?"

"Hell no. Her pussy was too damn good to go to sleep," he said, laughing at his own joke.

All I could do was shake my head because Kye was shot the fuck out. After we ate breakfast, he rode out to one of my warehouses with me. I had a few things to handle.

When I walked in the warehouse, the entire room fell silent. They already knew what it was. It was time for me to collect my money, then head to the airport. I had a quick flight to catch to Vegas to handle some business. Everybody put their bag of money one the table. I walked over to look inside each of them to make sure none of their punk asses wasn't trying to get over. Everybody's bag looked about right except Sean's. This nigga must have thought I was playing with his dumb ass.

"Sean, where the fuck is the rest of my money?" I asked calmly.

He started stuttering, so I knew he was about to come up with some bullshit. I pulled my gun out and shot that nigga in the head, and his body dropped to the floor. I was tired of playing games with these niggas. If you let them get away with one little thing, they would think you were soft and try you again.

I looked around the room to make sure I had everyone's attention. "Let this be a lesson to everyone standing here. If you fuck with my money and try to be bigger than me, I'll kill you without thinking twice," I warned before walking out the door with Kye on my heels.

"Nigga, your ass is as crazy as they come. You don't think about giving this shit up? You already have enough money that you won't be able to spend in this lifetime," he stated.

"I mean, yeah, I think about it from time to time, and eventually I will leave the game, be completely legit, and start a family. But for now, this is one of the things I wake up for," I told Kye, honestly.

"Damn, nigga, that's deep," was all he said.

We ended up going to grab some wings and shit and just chilled for a few hours. When I got home, I smoked a blunt, then went into my game room. I was in the mood to do some gaming for a few hours. Whenever I had some downtime, I played the game to clear my head. I was able to chill today since I didn't need to run to Vegas anymore.

For some reason, I couldn't get baby girl form the interview out of my head. I ain't never thought about a female the way I thought about her. I regret not hiring her. The chemistry was too thick for me to be around her regularly. I knew I would have started slipping. She was the type of woman that would make a nigga fall in love, and I wasn't ready for all of that.

I was horny as hell right about now. I'd been so busy that I hadn't fucked in about a week, and that wasn't like me. After my nap, I was going to go back to the city and get my dick wet by this chick named Mia. I fucked with her when I wanted some good ole' freaky shit. And that's what I was on tonight. I shot her a message to tell her what I wanted, and, of course, she was down. Getting a female was the easiest thing for me to do. Bitches wanted me just because of my status. And God forbid if I broke them off with some dick. They would do whatever I wanted. Once I texted her, I booked my room and took my ass to sleep.

Chapter Four

Andrea

"Welcome to Shyanne's. What can I do for you today?" the hairstylist asked when I sat in her chair.

"I want to try something new, but I don't know what to get, so I'm just going to trust your judgment," I told her.

"Girl, don't worry. I got you. I have the perfect style for you. By the way, this is no gay shit, but you are beautiful, and your skin is perfect," she complimented.

"Thanks, honey. You're pretty as well."

"Thanks, love."

After weeks of trying to find a way to get back in the company of Javier, we decided to try to go through his sister. It was a long shot, but it could work if I played my cards right. I decided to start up a conversation. "So how long have you been doing hair?"

"I've been playing in hair since I was a little girl, but I officially started five years ago when I opened up this salon."

"Oh, so you're, Shyanne, the owner?" I asked like I didn't already know the answer.

"Yes, I am. The one and only. What's your name?" she asked while walking me over to wash my hair.

"My name is Kamyra."

As she did my hair, we talked about a little bit of everything. I was enjoying her conversation. For some reason, she and I clicked like we'd known one another forever. When Shyanne was finally finished with my hair, she passed me a mirror. When I looked at myself, I was in disbelief on how some hair color and a little cut could change your entire appearance. I was feeling this style. She layered it and gave me the perfect shade of red to complement my skin complexion.

"I love it Shyanne. This complements my skin so well. I even like the length. You are officially my new hairstylist," I told her.

"Girl, this is why I do what I do. I love to make clients happy. You look even more beautiful now than you did when you walked in, and I didn't even think that was possible," she stated while stroking my hair.

I know she said she wasn't gay, but it was something about the way she complimented me. On my way out the door, Shyanne stopped me.

"Hey, I know this is a little unprofessional, but you should come out to my brother's lounge with me tonight."

"You know what? Why not? I could use some fun. Take my number and text me the address; I'll meet you there," I told her before heading to my car.

As soon as I got in, I called my captain to let him know what was going on, and, of course, he was excited. I went home and relaxed a little bit before hitting the lounge. I knew I was going to need a nap because my old ass hadn't been out, or had much of social life, in I don't know how long.

My phone buzzed, indicating that I had a text. When I looked at it, it was Shyanne sending me the address.

*****

I pulled up to the lounge that I not so long ago applied for and was shockingly rejected. When I got out the car, the men instantly started whistling. One dude had the nerve to grab my arm, and I damn near punched him in his face. That was the one thing I didn't play was a nigga touching me without my permission. I got to the font of the club just in time. Shyanne was just about to walk in. The line to the club was long, and I was glad I didn't have to wait in it thanks to my new "friend." When we walked in, Shyanne was greeted by all the workers, then we were taken to a VIP section.

When we got to the booth, we already had bottles up here. The music had me ready to get my dance on, but I needed to relax a little. First, I had to scope out the place and watch my surroundings. I decided to keep it simple and classy and ordered a cocktail. Javier and another very nice-looking guy walked into the room, and I damn near lost my breath. I knew I would see him here tonight, but I wasn't expecting my reaction to his presence. I gave myself a silent pep talk to keep my cool.

"Hey, bro. What's good? This is my friend, Kamyra. Kamyra, this is my brother, Javier," Shyanne introduced.

Javier and I just stared at one another for a few moments before speaking.

"I know you," he said.

"Yeah, you're the guy that decided not to give me a job, then put me out of your club without so much of an explanation," I replied.

"Wait, y'all two know each other?" Shyanne quizzed.

"I won't say we know one another, but we have met. I came for an interview, but this young man told me that my resume was impressive, yet he couldn't hire me. He didn't even have the decency to interview me or tell me why he didn't want to hire me," I said seriously.

"Damn, bro. Why didn't you hire her?" Shyanne pried.

"I didn't hire her because she's fucking beautiful and made my dick hard and my heart race a little faster. Like she's doing right now. I knew I couldn't work with her because she would be a distraction," Javier answered seriously, never breaking eye contact with me.

"Damn, bro. That's some serious shit coming from you. I can't lie, she is bad as fuck. If I was into girls, I would have tried to wife her," Shyanne stated with a giggle.

They were talking like I wasn't even standing here. I wasn't sure how to respond to either of them because I was too busy worrying about the juices that were wetting my panty liner.

"I appreciate the compliment, but are you telling me that you didn't hire me because I was too beautiful?" I quizzed.

"Yeah, but you missed the other reason, which was the important one. You make my dick hard, and my heart race. So, it was either not hire you, or hire you, and fuck the shit out of you every chance that I could. So, I chose a more professional option. Now I would like to change the subject. How do you know my sister?" he stated seriously.

I stood there feeling overwhelmed and speechless. I knew then that this undercover thing wasn't the job for me because I couldn't get caught up with a guy like Javier. "We met at her salon," I answered shyly. "I wanted a new look."

"You looked great before you changed your hair, but I must say, I'm feeling this style even better. Well, y'all ladies enjoy yourselves. I have a few things I need to do, but I'll be back," he stated before walking off.

His friend didn't leave right away. Instead, he sat and talked privately with Shyanne for a moment before getting up and leaving. Shyanne and I shared small talk and danced. Surprisingly, I was enjoying myself.

I was finally home, and I couldn't wait to get out of my heels because my feet were killing me. Something happened that caused Javier to leave in a hurry. I noticed that he, along with a few other guys that looked like bodyguards, rushed out. He sent his friend Kye to get Shyanne. I wasn't sure what was going on, but I hoped when I asked Shyanne about it that she would tell me. Just from the little interaction that I saw from her and Javier, let me know that they were close.

I laid in bed thinking about Javier. It was something about him. I could tell that he was cold and could murder someone without thinking twice about it. I finally drifted off to sleep.

When I woke up the next morning, I drove to the meetup spot to talk to the Captain. He wanted to be briefed on every little detail. I sat in my car and waited for him to pull up. When he got here, he got in my car.

"So, do you have any news for me?" he asked.

"Not really, but listen. I don't think I'm the right person for the job. He admitted to not hiring me because I make his dick hard and his heart race, and if he would have hired, me he would have fucked me every chance he got."

Captain's eyes damn near popped out of his head. "He said that? If so, you're the perfect one for the job," he stated with a sly smile.

"Captain, you don't understand. I also have a strong connection to him. I know it's weird, and I'm here to do a job, but I'm telling you that I don't think it's a good idea because I can't afford to jeopardize this case."

"Look, Andrea. You're staying on this case, and you'll do whatever needs to be done to bring this case to a close. I want him to spend the rest of his life behind bars. I don't give a damn if you have to marry his ass," he stated seriously. "You only have to do simple jobs to make him trust you and get information, and don't fall in love."

Yeah, that was the hard part, I thought to myself. I wasn't sure why he was so interested in Javier, but what I did know was, he wasn't going to let up until he put him behind bars.

"Whatever happens is on you," I stated honestly before he got out the car.

He looked back at me and said, "All I know is, you better not blow this case. Your entire career depends on it."

I was so pissed at his statement. I was about to pull off when my phone rang. When I saw it was Shyanne, I picked up.

"Hey, girl! What are you doing? You wanna grab some lunch?" she asked in one breath.

"Sure, why not? I'm starving."

"A'ight. I'm in the mood for pasta. How about Olive Garden?"

"Sounds good. I'll meet you there in about twenty minutes," I told her before disconnecting the call.

Chapter Five

Javier

Shit had been crazy for the last couple of weeks. The night Shyanne and Kamyra came to the club, somebody hit one of my stash spots, and it was now war. I wasn't sure who the fuck was behind it, but they fucked with the wrong nigga. I hoped their asses already brought their mommas' a black dress because I was going to bury whoever did it. I upped my security team just in case anything popped off at the home front. I made sure my sister was good, as well as my parents. Not that I had to do that because my dad could handle himself.

I barely had time to be at the club because I had to handle my street beef first. After trying to find out who crossed me on my own, I decided to put a million-dollar reward out for anyone that could prove that they knew who robbed me. The crazy thing was, they'll only get two hundred grand, but it was the principle. I knew I'd hear something soon.

I couldn't get Kamyra of my brain. It was something about her that drew me in, but I couldn't figure out what it was. Kamyra had a rear beauty and a nice ass body to go with it. I didn't like how she made me feel, and I had a feeling that I was going to be seeing her more than I intended to since she and my sister were now friends. I wasn't sure if that was a coincidence, or if something fishy was going on. All I knew was, it was something about her that I couldn't shake.

My cell ringing brought me from my thoughts. When I looked at my phone, it was Seth calling. Seth was like the head of my team. He reminded me of myself, so I trusted him more than I did the others.

"Yo', Seth, wassup?"

"I got some info that I think you would want to hear," he told me.

"A'ight, bet. Meet me at my club in half hour," I told him before disconnecting the call.

I pulled up to my club, and not too long after, Seth was pulling up behind me. He got out of his car and got in mine.

"Hey, boss. Listen, a cat named Marvin reached out and said he knows who hit your spot and that he wanted to meet with you to discuss some business. He said he knows there's a million-dollar reward, but he wants something less than what you're willing to pay. He gave me his number to give you to set up a meeting."

I looked at Seth with the side-eye because that didn't sound right to me. I took the number and called dude right away because I needed to know what the fuck he had going on. We decided to meet in two hours, but I was going to be there an hour earlier so I could watch and scope some shit out.

Dude pulled up twenty minutes before the scheduled time. He looked around to check out his surroundings before getting out his car to sit on the park bench. I finally decided to walk over and join him and see what he was talking about.

"What's good? I'm Javier," I stated, taking a seat with Seth standing beside me.

I had a few others in the parking lot watching as well. I rarely traveled alone because I knew niggas was out to get me. Don't get it fucked up. I could handle my own and didn't have an ounce of pussy in me. I was prepared to die if that's what it was gonna be because that's what happened when you was in the game.

"I'm Marvin. Listen, I know who hit your spot. Your boy Sean that works for you is working for a cat named Spence. Spence is out to get you something serious. He's a slimy ass nigga. He paid Sean fifty stacks to double-cross you, and Sean fell for it. The plan was to get you for all he could get, but they're banking on your big shipment that's coming in next month. Once they got the shipment, they planned to kill you and Sean's dumb ass," Marvin told me.

I took in everything that he said before speaking. "So, what's your role in this, and how do you know all this information? What do you want besides the million dollars that I'm offering?" I asked.

"My cousin, which I'm not naming, is fucking with Spencer's baby mom, and she is running her mouth every time he breaks her off with some dick and a little bit of cash. You know how these thirsty hoes are, and I'm telling you this because I can't stand that nigga Spence. I have been wanting him dead. He killed my little brother a few years ago."

"So why that nigga still breathing? And you didn't answer my question. What the fuck do you want for the information if you don't want the money? Even though you dun' already spilled the beans, so I don't have to give you shit or continue with the conversation," I replied honestly.

"I've done my research, and you not that type of guy to just off me for no reason. Besides, all I gave you was the first name. You don't know shit else, and the reason that nigga is still breathing is because I don't have the man power to kill his ass myself. He doesn't even know who I am. I was doing a bid when he got murdered.

"Spence is hard to get close to, but from what I get is, you more powerful than his ass, which is why he needs you out the game. All I'm asking is that you let me and my cousin join your crew. Let us work for you. I promise you won't regret it. We just want to eat and make it to the top," he stated.

Seth and I looked at one another before laughing in the dude's face.

"Nigga why the fuck should I trust you and let you work for me?"

"You shouldn't trust me. Just like I shouldn't trust you. I guess you're just gonna have to see if I'm trustworthy or not," he stated.

I had a pretty good read on people, and he seemed like a straight-up guy. I wasn't sure about the cousin. I would have to meet him. I did need another person on the team since Sean's ass was dead.

"A'ight, I'm gonna give you a shot, but one fuck up and I'll kill your ass. But as far as your cousin, I'll need to meet him. I'll give you info on a need to know bases. Be by your phone. I'll be in touch, but if you snooze, you lose," I told him before walking off.

As soon as I got in the car, I called one of my guys that I already had out there and put him on surveillance until further notice.

When I got home, I went to my office and lit a blunt. I decided to check my emails and my social media. Against my better judgment, I searched Kamyra's name and went through her profile. She had a nigga tripping on her, and she hadn't even done anything. I knew I couldn't cross the line with her because I would have to kill a nigga just for looking at her.

My parents called me last night to let me know that they were back in town and to tell me that they were having a party next week. They through the best parties with some very important people, so I knew I couldn't wait. Besides, I missed my parents. I called Kye to tell him to make sure he came to the festivity with me.

******

Later that night, I went to my club to see how shit was running. Surprisingly, it was super packed for a Thursday night. I went into my office and did the payroll, and once I was finished, I decided I was in the mood to get my dick wet. I called up this chick named Trisha to meet me at the club.

"Hey, daddy," she cooed into the phone.

"You already know what time it is, ma. Bring your ass to the club. Throw on something sexy and skip the panties," I told her before hanging up the phone.

I went to the bathroom and washed off. I had to make sure my dick was clean. As instructed, Trisha walked into my office with a sexy robe on and a pair of heels. Nothing else; just as I instructed her to do.

"Hey, daddy. I missed you. What took you so long to call me?"

"Enough with all the talking. Bring your ass over here and show a nigga how much you missed this dick," I replied, not beat for all the small talk. I sat on the couch that I had in my office and watched as Trisha crawled on her knees to come to bless me with a good dick suck. "Fuck, girl, suck this big dick," I told her while guiding her head up and down on my rock-hard dick.

Trisha's head game was serious. She had me reaching for shit that wasn't even there. I was ready to feel the pussy. I pulled her head back so I could get up. I slid a condom on, then bent her ass over the couch and started fucking her like that shit was going out of style.

"Oh, fuck, daddy, this dick feels good!" Trisha moaned loudly, making my dick even harder.

I grabbed a handful of her hair and went into beast mode until I nutted in the condom. I walked in the bathroom and wiped myself off. I brought her out a rag so she could do the same.

"That was good as fuck, daddy," she said, running her hands down my chest. "Javier, when are you going to stop playing and make me your girl?"

I just knew I heard her wrong. I spent my head around so fast I thought I caught whiplash. "Tisha, I don't know what the fuck you on tonight, but I know you bullshitting. You and I will never be together, so don't ever come at me like that again," I told her seriously.

"Damn, daddy. You don't have to be so rude about it. I was just saying maybe we should be together. I know you like me more than you're willing to admit."

"Trisha, I don't know where you getting this, 'I like you' bullshit from, but I don't even know you to like you. All we do is fuck. I won't be calling you again, so I hope you enjoyed the dick because this was the last time. Have a great life, Trisha." I was holding the door open for her to leave.

I hated that I had to treat her like that after the nut she just gave me, but I had to put her ass in her place. I wasn't wifeing none of these hoes. They had the game fucked up.

After that, I had I decided to stay at my house in Camden for the night. Trisha had to fuck up a good thing. I couldn't understand why chicks always needed to change the status of shit.

Once my driver, Dion, dropped me off, I took a shower and took my ass to bed. I didn't even bother to eat anything. I laid in the bed and stared at the ceiling thinking about today's events. I had to figure out what I was gonna do about Marvin and his cousin. He seemed like a straight-up guy, but I didn't trust anyone. I sent his info to my private investigator earlier today, and he told me he should have some info for me by noon tomorrow.

My phone ringing woke me up from my sleep. I looked at the clock on my nightstand, and it was only eight o'clock in the morning. I grabbed my phone, and it was the private investigator, so I knew he must have had some info. "Talk to me," I said as soon as I picked up.

"I got that info you asked for. Dude seems to be legit. He was locked up at the time his brother was killed. The guy, Spence, does seem to be hard to get at and is feared by many. But check this out. I found out some even more interesting news about the dude Spence. He has a brother named Sean Wilson."

When he said that, my eyes got wide as hell because that meant all hell was about to break loose. I knew that sean was working with him but I didn't know that was his brother now I knew I was gonna have to kill this nigga ASAP. I had just killed Sean, and he probably knew more about my business than he should have.

"Thanks. I'll send over your payment now," I told him before hanging up.

I sent the crew a text letting them know we had a meeting in an hour. I got up and took a shower and threw some clothes on so I could go set a plan in motion. I had so many thoughts running through my head. Sean had been working for me for a few years now, and it made me wonder how long he had been crossing me.

Chapter Six

Shyanne

"Fuck, Kye. I swear you got some good dick. If I would have known your dick was this good, I would have been giving you some pussy," I expressed when he rolled off of me.

Kye and I had been fucking for two weeks now. Ever since the night Javier had him take me home from the club to be exact. I was falling pretty hard for Kye, but I knew I had to keep my feelings in check. My parents would probably die if they found out about us, and Javier would probably kill me and Kye. Kye and I were considered family in our parents' eyes, but I've always thought that Kye was fine as hell. We were brought up together, so he and I were just as close as him and Javier.

"Shy, you better stop talking like that before I put this dick back in you," he stated cockily.

"As tempting as that sounds, I have to get to the shop because I have a client in less than an hour."

With that, I got up from the bed to shower. Of course, Kye joined me, and that turned into a quickie I didn't want to end, but I couldn't be late and have my client waiting. I loved dick, but I was about my bag first.

"You're lucky that's all we had time for because I would have been knee-deep in that pussy all damn day. Yo', we need to tell Javier we fucking around."

His statement damn near caused me to lose my breath. "Kye we can't tell him, or anyone for that matter. Javier would never be okay with us fucking, and you know our parents will have a heart attack," I replied honestly.

"Shyanne, I'm a grown-ass man and can do as I please. If you think I'm about to be some secret lover at night and be your play brother during the day, then you got the game fucked up. As a matter of fact, don't hit my line until you figure out what you want to do. I'm out," he stated angrily before storming out the door.

Unfortunately, I couldn't worry about Kye's feelings right now. I had to get to work.

On the way to work, I thought about the day I caught Jeff fucking in my house. I killed both of them without thinking twice about it. I kind of missed Jeff, but he should have known better than to cross me.

I finally pulled up to my shop, and when I walked in, Kamyra was already being shampooed. Kamyra and I became pretty close pretty, quick. I think that my brother has a thing for her, but he wouldn't admit to it. I saw the way he was looking at her the night we were at the club.

Once she was done being shampooed, she hopped in my chair.

"Hey, girl, wassup?" I spoke when she sat down.

"Hey, girl. Not much is up with me. I've just been chilling. Me and my boyfriend broke up. It just wasn't working," she replied.

"Damn, girl. I'm sorry to hear that. I have the perfect idea to help you cheer up. My parents are throwing a party tomorrow night, and I think you should come."

"You sure they wouldn't mind?"

"I'm sure. A friend of mine is a friend of theirs," I told her.

"Okay, I guess it won't hurt to get out the house," she agreed.

After I was done with her hair, I gave her a mirror, and she liked it. That was all I needed to hear. I loved to make my clients happy. She also wanted me to do her toes and nails. I couldn't lie if I wanted to. Kamyra was perfect. I swear if I was into women, I would have been eating her pussy on my desk right about now.

"Just make sure you wear something formal."

"Okay, cool. I have plenty of dresses. I'll see you tomorrow text me the address," she said before walking out the salon.

I was glad the day was finally over and I could go home because I needed a nap. I didn't get much sleep fucking around with Kye all night. Thinking about last night had me thinking about him. I pulled out my cell and called him. To my surprise, he answered on the first ring.

"Shyanne, if you haven't made up your mind, then you need to hang up."

I pulled the phone back from my ear and looked at it with my face ripped up. Kye must have lost his damn mind. "Kye, I know you not feeling what I said to you earlier, but you need to watch how you talk to me. I am not one of your little hoes."

"That's funny that you say you don't want me to talk to you like you're a hoe, but you want to act like one and treat me like some side nigga. Shyanne, what do you want?"

I took a deep breath before speaking because I didn't feel like going back and forth with him. "Can you please just come over tonight so we can talk? Please?" I asked.

"A'ight Shyanne. You better make it worth my wild," he said before hanging up.

Kye was a piece of work. I couldn't handle him the way I handled other men that I dealt with because he was ruthless and cutthroat just like me and Javier. We were raised by drug dealers and killers, so that shit ran deep in our veins and we couldn't help it.

*****

Later that evening, I was taking a relaxing bath when my phone buzzed, letting me know that I had a text message. When I opened my phone, it was a text from Kye telling me to unlock the door because he was on his way. I climbed out of the tub and dried off so I could let him in. After I opened the door, I went and slipped into something comfortable and sexy.

"Shy, where you at?" Kye's sexy ass voice called when he walked into the house.

"I'm up here, Kye."

I knew we were just supposed to talk, but when Kye walked in the room, my pussy starting throbbing, and all I wanted to do was feel him deep inside of me.

"So, what do you want to talk about, Shyanne?"

I knew he was still pissed because he called me by my name. Kye had been calling me Shy since we were kids.

"Look, Kye. I'm sorry about how I spoke to you earlier, but please let me explain. I'm not ready to out us yet before we even know where we're headed. We've only been fucking around for a couple of weeks. You know if we tell everyone about us right now, before we even know what we are, it'll be even more messy. We haven't even talked about us yet, because every time we see each other we, start ripping off one another's clothes. Not to mention the fact that they see us like family, so good luck explaining what we have going on."

"A'ight, Shyanne. I'm gonna hold off before saying anything, but it won't be for long. You're the one that needs to figure out what you want from me. Because before that night after the club, I already knew what I wanted. I know you just as well as I know myself, so what's to figure out? You looking good right now, and as much as I want to hit that, I have to run. But thanks for the talk. I'll holler at you later," he said before walking out.

I laid on my bed and let out a heavy sigh. I didn't know what to do about Kye, but he was right about everything that he said.

Chapter Seven

Andrea

I'd just got back from meeting with the Captain. I had to let him know about my invitation to the party. I was starting to get upset, and I wanted to be off of this case more and more every day. I couldn't understand why Javier wouldn't give me the time of day. I was beautiful and successful with a body to die for, yet he would barely even look at me.

I lied to Shyanne about having plenty of formal dresses. The truth was, I didn't own a single formal dress, but I had a credit card curtesy of my Captain. Hell, I had my own money, but why should I buy my shit for work? I decided to hit up a boutique in Collingswood to grab me a few dresses. I wanted to make a hell of a impression tonight.

After shopping for a few hours, I had everything that I needed, including dresses, shoes, and handbags to go with them. My hair was already done, so I didn't have much more to do. When I got home, I kicked off my shoes and just relaxed on the couch for a bit. I couldn't stop thinking about this case and all the ways it might play out. I know I baited Shyanne so I could try to get close to Javier, but the truth was, I liked her, and we're starting to get pretty close.

I was finally dressed and looking like a million bucks. I had to change my outfit from what I originally was going to wear because Shyanne texted me to tell me that her parents wanted it to be an all-black affair, which I was cool with. I looked in the mirror and I looked perfect. I was wearing a long, black, off-the-shoulder gown with a midway split that showed off my black and silver pumps. I wore my hair in a bun with two strands loose on each side.

I went with silver jewelry and a handbag. I applied my lip gloss to my lips, and I was ready to go. Shyanne told me not to worry about the address because she was going to pick me up. She told me her parents were sending her a car over so she wouldn't have to drive. I was excited to meet the parents of Javier and Shyanne Santos. The Santos name rang bells in the streets, so I was ready to see what all the noise was about. Shyanne texted and told me to come out. When I got outside, it was a long, stretched, black limo waiting.

******

We drove for about twenty-five minutes before arriving at her parents' house. When we pulled up, I couldn't help but drop my mouth open. I was at a freaking mansion. This was shit that you saw on TV but not real life. To say I was in awe was an understatement. The driver came around and opened the door for me and Shyanne. When I stepped out, I fixed my hair, and I applied some more lip gloss. For some reason, I was suddenly nervous and could feel the butterflies doing backflips in my stomach. *Breathe, Andrea, breathe*, I silently coached myself.

"Damn, Kamyra. You look stunning," Shyanne stated, breaking me from my thoughts.

"Thanks, Shyanne. You look stunning as well. This place is freaking huge."

"Girl, wait until you see the inside. My place is big, but nothing compared to this. Javier's place may be just a tad smaller, but not by much," she stated like that shit was regular.

When we got inside, I was in disbelief about how nice it was. Again, this was shit you only saw on TV. Everyone looked amazing in their black attire. I looked around to see if I could find Javier, but I didn't see him. I didn't want to ask Shyanne about him because I didn't want her to know that I was checking for him.

"Come on. I want you to meet my parents," Shyanne said, grabbing my arm.

I couldn't believe how much Shyanne looked like her mom.

"Hey, Mom and Dad. I want you to meet my close friend, Kamyra. Kamyra, this is my mom, Shanice, and my dad, Franklin," she introduced.

Her mother was a beautiful woman with long hair that came to the middle of her back. Her mom surprisingly hugged me, and her father kissed the back of my hand. He was also a very handsome man, and it was evident where Javier got his looks from.

"Hello, Kamyra. It's nice to meet you. You're beautiful," Mrs. Shanice stated as she took in my appearance.

"Hey, fam," I heard a voice say.

When I turned around, I was staring in the eyes of none other than Javier. I took in his appearance, and he was wearing a black suit, you could tell was customized, with a white shirt and a black and white bow tie. The pair of black and white shoes on his feet looked expensive.

"Hello, Kamyra. You look stunning," he stated, never breaking his stare.

"Hello, Javier. You're looking pretty stunning, yourself."

Javier gently grabbed my hand and kissed the back of it, just as his father did. But I wasn't expecting what he did next. He placed one of my fingers in his mouth and seductively sucked on it—like it was just the two of us in the room. As bad as I wanted to pull back, it felt too good to stop him. My panties were already moist just at the sight of him.

Javier's father cleared his throat. "Son, don't you think that's a bit much to be doing in front of your parents and little sister?"

"Nah, I don't, actually. I think it's time for me to get to know Ms. White. They say three time's a charm, and this is the third time that I've been blessed with her presence. And every time I see her, she does something to me that no woman has ever done before."

"And what might that be son?" his mother cut in and asked.

I stood waiting to hear the damn answer, myself. I might have been able to ask the question on my own if I wasn't standing here stuck.

"She makes my heart flutter is what she does," Javier answered, staring me directly in my eyes.

This shit was like a movie. The feeling was unrealistic. The room fell silent for a few moments.

"Can I speak to you two in private?" Javier's mother asked, catching me off guard.

I couldn't think of anything that she could want to talk to us about. Javier grabbed my hand as we walked behind his parents. When we got into the lavish room, his mother didn't waste any time getting to the point.

"Javier, I've never seen you behave or speak about a woman like this before, which lets me know how far gone you already are. Does she know what you do for a living?" she asked with raised eyebrows.

He gave her a keep quiet look, but she didn't pay any attention to his pleading eyes. I had to step in and say something because they were acting as if I wasn't in the room.

"Yes, ma'am, I do. He owns a night club," I answered.

Ms. Shanice laughed in my face, and I couldn't understand what the hell was so damn funny.

"I'll take that as a no. My son's night club is just one of the small things he does as a hobby, but his real job is dealing drugs. That's right, my son is one of the biggest kingpins out there."

"Mom, why would you tell her something like that?"

"Yes, what the hell do you think you're doing?" Javier's father chimed in, not sounding too happy about what his wife had disclosed.

I was in utter shock that she said something like that to me the first time meeting me.

"Look, it's apparent that he's feeling this young lady, and she needs to know what he does and what she's going to be getting herself into. He needs to make sure she can handle that. Being with a kingpin ain't no easy job. Now that you know what he does, can you handle it? Is being with a kingpin something that you want? I'm not trying to scare you off, I just want to give you the facts. If it was up to these men, you wouldn't know anything until it's too late."

"And what if she runs and tells the cops?" Javier asked.

Only if he knew I *was* the cops. I hadn't even started anything with him, and I already felt like I was in way over my head. But I had a job to do, so this was the time to play my part.

"I wasn't aware that he was a kingpin. However, with all due respect, we've only briefly been in one another's presence a few short times, and I don't feel like that was my business. But now that you have made it my business, I guess I should address it. I can handle whatever he brings to the table. He must be a very powerful man if he's one of the largest kingpins out there, and, yet, he's still on the streets. If I ever decided to take to being more than anything but an acquaintance of Mr. Santos, I'm a big girl and can handle myself, but thanks for the concern. If that's all, then I would like to enjoy the party. By the way, you guys have a lovely home," I stated before exiting the room.

I made sure to add a little extra to my walk as I left out, knowing they all would be watching. Once I made my way back to the party, I scanned the room for Shyanne, which I found on the dance floor slow dragging with the guy that I believe was Javier's best friend. I stood on the side and waited for them to finish. I was hungry and ready to eat. Javier's parents now had a microphone and requested everyone's attention.

"Good evening, everyone. My wife and I would like to thank each one of you for coming out to party with us tonight. We're going to have a wonderful time. But for now, let's eat," Mr. Franklin announced.

Everyone started walking off to another room. We walked into a giant dining area that was set up nicely. I almost felt like I was at a wedding or a ball. I wasn't sure what the occasion was for the party, but what I could say was, the Santos sure knew how to throw a party and entertain their guest.

Chapter Eight

Javier

Shit couldn't have been going better between me and Kamyra. We'd been hanging out and chilling for a little over a month now, and surprisingly, we hadn't had sex yet. For the first time in my life, I wasn't even worried about that shit right now. I was feeling Kamyra and could see myself settling down with her. Kamyra and my sister were the best of friends, and I was loving every minute of it. My parents also liked Kamyra as well. They said they loved the way she handled herself at the party.

To be honest, that was the night that I said fuck it and decided to go all-in with Kamyra. She was looking hella good that night. Not to mention how sexy it was to watch her put my mom in her place. What made it sexy was, she did it with respect. I loved my mom to death, but she could be a bit much sometimes with very few people willing to tell her about herself. From that encounter, I could tell that wasn't the case with Kamyra.

"Javier, Kye is here to see you," Ms. Claire said through the intercom.

"Yo', nigga, wassup?" Kye said when he walked in.

"Shit. About to handle some shit at the warehouse before I meet up with Kamyra."

"Damn, nigga. I never thought I'd see the day when your ass would be all in love and shit. That pussy must be fire," he stated.

"I'm feeling, baby girl. She's gonna be my wife, but to be honest, I haven't even fucked her yet."

Kye's eyes looked like they were about to pop out of his head. "What the fuck you mean you haven't hit it yet?" he quizzed.

"Just what I said. I'm not off that right now. Just know once I put this dick in her, it's a wrap. She's gonna be mine forever because I refuse to believe someone that looks that good has whack pussy," I said with a chuckle.

"Damn, nigga, that's deep," was all he could say.

Me and Kye chilled at my crib for about an hour before I had to head out. I had an appointment meeting, and I couldn't be late.

*****

"Hey, beautiful. I've missed you all day. How was your day?" I asked, placing a kiss on her lips.

"My day was pretty good. How was yours?" she replied, returning the kiss.

After kissing for what seemed like forever, we finally pulled apart. I was on my way taking my baby out to do a little shopping, and then out to eat. We had reservations at eight tonight at some fancy restaurant that just opened up not too far from my house. On our way shopping, my phone ringing brought me from my thoughts.

"Yo', wassup?" I answered.

"Yo', we have a fucking problem and need you to get here ASAP!"

"A'ight, I'm on my way," I said before disconnecting the call.

The urgency in his voice let me know that shit was serious. I had to get to the warehouse as soon as possible but, I didn't want to take Kamyra with me. Especially since I didn't know what the fuck was going on. I would never forgive myself if something happened to her on my watch.

"Listen, baby, I have an emergency at the warehouse, and I usually would never do this, but I need you to ride with me," I told her.

"Okay, baby," she said.

I was shocked about how calm she was. We pulled up to the warehouse in forty-five minutes with the speed I was driving. Before I got out of the car, I pulled out my cell and logged in so I could see what was going on in there. I always had to know what I was walking into. I could see three niggas holding guns to my worker's heads. I shot my other workers a text, letting them know what was up before heading in. When I got out of the car, Kamyra got out with me, and I looked at her like she was crazy.

"Are you crazy? You can't go in there with me. I have no idea what I'm walking into," I told her.

"I'm not staying out here. What if somebody snatches me out of the car or something? I think I'm safer with you than without you."

Kamyra was right, so against my better judgment, I let her walk in with me.

I walked into the warehouse with a guns in hand, making sure I gave Kamyra protection as well. Just like on ,my security monitor, we walked in on three niggas holding guns to my worker's heads. When I happened to look down, I saw one of my worker's head cut off. I wasn't sure what the fuck had happened, or how my workers allowed this shit to happen. Nor was I sure if I was going to make it out of here alive, but I knew I was going to die trying. However, my biggest concern at this point was making sure Kamyra was good. I looked at her, and she squeezed my hand, but for some reason, she didn't seem to be as afraid as I thought she would be.

"I'm not sure who the fuck you are, or what the fuck you want, but it's apparent that y'all niggas were waiting on me. So now that I'm here, speak your fucking mind," I stated, ready for whatever.

One of the guys turned his gun on me and started laughing. That was a big no for me. My rule was simple: you point a gun at, me you better kill me. The nigga holding the gun was about to speak but couldn't get a word in before a bullet crashed through his head. Everyone was looking to see who the shooter was as they started blasting off.

I had my warehouse set up with guns in places that you would never even imagine a gun could be. Guns could either be operated by my voice or a special keychain that I had made. A bullet came flying in my direction, so I pushed Kamyra to the floor as a bullet pierced through my shoulder. As she slid across the floor, she was now busting off with guns in her hand. She shot one of the guys in the head, and his body hit the floor hard. At this point, we were in a full gun blaze.

This shit was crazy. I was now able to get my gun out but not before I was shot again. I wasn't sure who had shot me because all the men that were in the warehouse were already down, but when I looked up, another big nigga had walked in. I was shot in a few places at this point and wasn't sure if I was going to live or die. I saw my worker, Reem, walk over to the guy that had just shot me, and they exchanged a few words. Now I was confused because I know this motherfucker didn't set me up.

"You're not so tuff now is you, Javier? This about to be my empire," Kareem said with a stupid ass chuckle.

I couldn't believe this shit. Why the fuck would he cross me like this? I was nothing but good to this motherfucker.

"Nigga, fuck you," I spat. If I was going to die, I was still going to go out like a man.

"Give me the code to the safe, or you and this bitch will die," Kareem threatened, holding a gun to Kamyra' s head. That nigga went on and on about he and were in this together and how I was about to loose everything.

I felt like shit not being able to protect her as I should have. The look she was wearing was one that I was familiar with. She didn't look scared. Hell, she barley acted like she was even bothered. It was more like a reassurance that everything was gonna be okay, but I wasn't too sure about that. Before I could even respond, Kamyra did some shit that had me looking at her ass like she was crazy. She elbowed dude in the neck, then slid on her ass backwards, drawing two guns from her boots and started blasting off. Kareem's brains splattered on the walls. I was able to shoot the other guy, then everything went black.

******

I woke up in the hospital connected to an IV and a tube in my nose. As soon as I started to move around, I opened my eyes. My mom, Dad, Shyanne, and Kye were sitting in chairs. Once my eyes were fully open, I tried to talk, but my mouth was dry as shit.

"Oh my God, son, you're awake," my mom said as everyone crowded around my bed.

But the one person that was on my mind was the one person I didn't see.

"Where's Kamyra?" I mustered up enough strength to say.

I just hoped they didn't tell me that she was dead because I wouldn't have been able to live with myself if something happened to her on my watch. Before anyone could answer, the room door opened, and in walked Kamyra. I was so happy to see her beautiful face. When she realized I was awake, she ran over and kissed me like we were the only two in the room, causing the machine to go off.

"I thought you were dead," I said with tears running down my face. I knew I was tripping because Kamyra had me crying at the sight of her. I'd never had any emotion for any woman in my life before, let alone cried over one.

After talking to the doctors and my family for a few, I wanted to take a nap. The doctors said that I would make a full recovery and that the bullets didn't damage any main organs. I just couldn't wait to get out of the hospital. My pops had around the clock security and said he wasn't going to rest until someone paid for what they did. I knew he meant it. And I was ready for the war.

Chapter Nine

Andrea

"Andrea, have you lost your damn mind? You could have died! Why did you think it was a bright idea for you to get involved in a damn shootout? Are you trying to blow this damn case, Andrea? I hope you didn't fall in love with him, because at the end of this bust, you gonna get your feelings hurt! This is for pretend! This ain't no damn fairytale love story!" Captain yelled.

I was getting pissed and ready to curse his ass out. "What the hell was I supposed to do, Cap? We were together when it happened. I wasn't trying to die, and if I'm not mistaken, you need him alive, right? Besides, I tried to get off the case remember? I told you it was a bad idea. It's been damn near two months and today was the most excitement that I've seen. I still don't know anything more than what you've told me about this man. I haven't seen any drugs, nor have I heard him talk about drugs. So, for him to be some large kingpin, I don't see the fucking evidence. Now you put me on the case, so I need to move whatever way I see fit to close this case. And if that's not what you want, then take me off and find someone else," I snapped.

I knew some of my anger was personal because I had fallen for Javier, but at this point, I've told myself that I could walk away at any time. Nonetheless, I wasn't sure if I could do it if I kept going at this rate. I was trying my hardest to refrain from being intimate with Javier, and to be honest, the only reason we probably didn't have sex yet was because he never pushed the issue. I was surprised that he never made a sexual move on me at this point. The most we did was kiss.

I also felt like something was off with the Captain. He'd wanted Javier. To be honest, it almost felt like he had a personal vendetta against Javier, but he would never say it.

"Look, Andrea. Just do what you need to do to get this case closed, and I'm only giving you one more month to do so before I have to take matters in my hands," Captain stated in a serious tone.

It was something about his tone that didn't sit right with me. I didn't even bother to say anything. I just got out the car, checked my surroundings, and got in my car and peeled off.

I needed to talk to someone right now, and what better person than my best friend? I didn't even bother calling. I just drove straight to her house. When I pulled up, I was glad to see that her car was here. I got out and let myself in.

She sounded like she was on the phone, but when she realized I was here, she jumped like she had been caught doing something wrong.

"Hey, bestie. What you in here jumping for? I know your ass wasn't scared?"

"I just wasn't expecting you, that's all. It's been a minute since you've been over. But what's up with you? I missed my best friend. Are you any closer to closing the case?" Jessica asked.

"Girl, not one bit. He doesn't even talk about the drug business or money. But we did get into a shootout, and Javier almost lost his life."

Jessica's mouth fell open in surprise, and I'm sure she wanted to know every detail. I wasn't really allowed to discuss specifics, but she was my best friend, and she was also a cop. So I decided to tell her everything, including my feelings for Javier.

After we caught up for a few hours, I finally made my way home. I needed to clear my head because I just had a lot going on. I walked into the house and decided to take a nap because I was tired. I laid in the bed and stared up at the ceiling, replaying me and Captain's entire conversation. The more I thought about this case, the more I wanted it to be over with.

Before I dozed off, I thought about how slightly weird Jessica seemed when I was at her place. I wasn't sure what the hell was going on with everybody. I just knew that I needed some space to think.

My cell ringing caused me to jump up from my sleep. When I looked at the number, it wasn't one that I recognized, but I answered it anyway.

"Hello?" I said in a sleepy tone.

"Hey, beautiful. I didn't mean to wake you. I just missed you and needed to hear your voice," Javier said when I answered.

"Hey, Javier. How are you feeling?" I asked.

As much as I liked Javier, a part of me didn't want to talk to him right now. But I knew I had a job to do, so I had to find a way to separate my personal feelings.

"I'm just in a little pain right now, but I'm okay. Just can't wait to get out of here so I can handle some shit. I won't rest until those niggas pay for what they did to me. I'm in the game, so I expect for shit to pop off with me, but they gonna pay for putting the love of my life at risk," he ranted.

I took the phone from my ear and looked at it, not believing what he just said to me. I knew that he cared a lot about me, but I had no idea that I was the love of his life. I had feelings for him—way more than I should—but being in love was a bit much.

"Javier, you need to take it easy before you try to seek revenge. I'm sure you'll still be in pain even after you get released," I said, trying to change the subject.

I just hoped that he didn't bring it back up or acknowledge the fact that I didn't say it back.

"Listen, baby. I'll be just fine. You don't need to worry about me. It's my job to worry about you. But, baby, I'm about to get some sleep. I'll see you tomorrow."

"Okay, get some rest. I'll be up there tomorrow morning," I told him before hanging up the phone.

*****

It'd been a few weeks since Javier was shot. I had spent the last two weeks at his place nursing him back to health and taking care of some of the business at the club. Javier's house was just extravagant as his parents'. This was a house and life I could get used to. It was too bad this was all a sham and would soon be coming to an end. I swear I wished I could have met Javier in another lifetime. Things were pretty intense between us, yet we still hadn't had sex. I wasn't sure why he hadn't made a move on me yet, but a part of me was glad that he didn't. Because I could only imagine how much harder it would be to turn him in after fucking him. I often fantasized about what I thought it would be like. Javier didn't strike me as the lovemaking type of man. He came off as the fuck you crazy and turn your ass out type of guy.

The Captain was breathing down my neck harder and harder. He wasn't happy that this case was still open; not to mention that I wasn't any closer to bringing it to a close. Captain was reneging on his word for some reason. When he first put me on the case, he told me he didn't care how long it took or what I had to do. Now it was like he was rushing and acting like he wanted me to make something up.

"Hey, baby. What are you in here doing?" Javier asked me, breaking me from my thoughts.

"Not much. I was just checking some emails. Do you need me to do anything?"

"Nah, baby. I'm good. You've done more than enough already. But I would like for you to accompany me to Kye's surprise birthday party next week at my lounge. It will be closed to the public; just family and close friends," Javier stated, placing a kiss on my forehead.

"I would love to be your date, Mr. Santos," I flirted.

A few hours later, it was time for my hair appointment with Shyanne. I wanted her to dye my hair a different color. I was thinking about honey-blonde or something. Usually, I just let her do her, but today, I had some pictures of things that I wanted that I saw in a magazine. When I got to the shop, Shyanne wasn't there yet, but the shampoo girl washed my hair and sat me under the dryer. A few moments later, Shyanne sent me a text letting me know that she was running a little late.

So, I decided to stroll through my social media accounts: the real and the fake ones. Apart of me felt some type of way because I had more going on as Kamyra White than I did as Andrea Moore. I was just a police officer with no family and friends except Jessica, and I barley saw or talked to her like that. When I did, things still seemed a little weird to me. But as Kamyra white, I was associated with one the largest kingpins, and I was living a lavish life that I could get used to.

I had even managed to gain a great friend. One who I didn't want to lose, but I knew everyone would hate me, and I would possibly even be in danger. Tears filled my eyes as I sat and thought about the mess I was in. I wasn't sure that I could go through with it anymore. I was going to try to talk to the Captain once more to see if we could figure something else out.

I wasn't any closer to Javier's drug business, and I don't think it was because he didn't trust me. He was just private and careful with the way he moved. Yes, he had money, and I'd heard brief conversations, but everything was brief and kinda coded. I hadn't seen anything about him that could even get him a ticket, let alone arrested.

I was falling in love with Javier, and according to him, he was already in love. This was a mess, and I no longer wanted any parts of this mess. I also felt like it was time to do my research as to why the Captain wanted Javier so badly. We knew other big time drug dealers with proof of what they were doing, yet he wasn't worried about them. I was starting to feel like this was more personal than it was business.

Chapter Ten

Trevor

"Babe, you need to relax. This case has you going crazy. If you don't mind me asking, why is putting him behind bars so important to you? That's all you seem to talk about these days," Jessica asked.

"Look, Jessica. I don't want to talk about this right now. But I will say this. That damn Andrea is about to piss me off even more than she's already doing. All I asked was for her to help bring that nigga down, and she can't even do that. I thought she was would be the one that could get it done, but it sounds like her ass went and fell in love, and now she can't do her job. How the hell you been with this nigga for a little over three months and saying that you still don't know shit?"

"Trevor, what did you expect to happen? You got her down there playing house with a rich ass, nice-looking, powerful man. You know Andrea is single and alone. Bedsides me, she doesn't have anyone. I think that you're being a little hard on her, Trevor."

I thought about what Jessica said, and she was probably right, but I could care less if she was right or not. I wanted Javier Santos dealt with, and I wanted it done immediately.

And if she didn't do it soon, I was gonna have to take matters into my own hands.

"Look, let's just forget about it. I don't feel like talking about this anymore. You need to talk to your friend. Get dressed. We need to get ready for work," I told her.

"Trevor, how long are we supposed to keep our relationship a secret?"

"We don't need everyone at the station in our business. Plus, I could get into a lot of trouble for even dealing with you," I told Jessica honestly.

"Trevor, we've been together for six months, and I can't even tell my best friend about us. I feel like I'm creeping around with a married man or something."

"We gonna be late. We can talk about this later tonight over dinner. I'll make reservations somewhere nice," I promised. I kissed her on the lips before heading to take a shower.

My name is Trevor Jackson, and I'm the Captain at the Camden County Police Department. I loved my job but felt like I failed once my brother got killed. My brother chose the streets, and as much as I tried to convince him to go legit, he wouldn't listen. My brother's death was the reason why I wanted Javier Santos to be put in prison. Javier killed my brother a few years ago, but it wasn't enough evidence to have him arrested.

The truth was, as soon as he got to prison, I had some men on the inside that was gonna handle him for me. I was gonna have him tortured then killed. I wouldn't sleep peacefully until that nigga was six feet under. I knew I couldn't tell anyone that because they would know that I had a personal vendetta against him, which could fuck up the case. So, this was just my little secret.

******

It'd been a week since I'd heard anything from Andrea, and I was starting to get pissed. I told Andrea to report to me once a week at our spot, but this week, she didn't show up or answer her phone. I knew that her ass was good because she talked to Jessica. Me and Jessica started fucking around about six months ago. We went out for drinks one night after a long shift and had one too many drinks that led to a night of great sex. Once we sobered up, we vowed that we wouldn't do it again. But obviously, that was a lie, and we'd been messing around ever since. Over the past six months, I eventually developed real feelings for her.

I honestly wanted Andrea. She was beautiful, smart, and had a body to die for. Since the moment she walked into this station, I wanted her. But I knew she would never cross that line with me because I was friends with her father. We worked a few cases together, so she looked at me as a father-figure. But fuck that. I wanted to fuck the shit out of Andrea. I knew if I got in the pussy that it was a wrap. I would fuck around and marry her ass. Thoughts of Javier putting his dick in Andrea made me sick to my stomach. Just the thought had me ready to pull her off this case.

"Babe, I'm leaving. I'll see you at work," Jessica said, bringing me from my thoughts. I kissed her on her lips before walking her to her car.

I walked back in the house and grabbed the rest of my things. When I got in the car, I called Andrea's ass once more, and, of course, she didn't answer. She was starting to piss me off with ignoring my calls. When I got into work, I had a shit load of paperwork to do. So I walked into my office, took a few sips of my coffee, and got to work. A few hours into the workday, my phone rang. It was Andrea. I picked up on the first ring.

"What the hell is your problem—" I started to say, but was cut off.

"Just meet me at the spot," she said into the phone and hung up before I could reply.

Andrea's ass was getting out of hand. She had me fucked up if she thought she was going to do what she wanted when it came to this case. I jumped in my car and sped off. When I got to the spot, Andrea was already there. When she saw my car pulling up, she got out of the car and sat on the hood of her car. I walked over to where she was parked and laid her ass out.

"What the hell happened to you Andrea? I've been calling you all damn week. I told you to report to me every damn week; not when you feel like it!" I snapped.

"Listen here, Captain. I have a lot of respect for you, especially since you were a friend of my father, but I don't know who the fuck you think you're talking to like that. I'm not sure if you have kids or not, but what I do know is, I ain't the fuck one of them. But if you must know, I've been staying at Javier's house all week and can't be creeping around on the phone with you. As I told you before, I still don't have shit.

"So, I've come to a few conclusions about this. One: take me off the case because this man either is not as big of a drug dealer as you think he is, or he's just careful. Either way, that doesn't help us not one bit, and if you're going to be breathing down my neck, give the job to someone else. I can't give you information that I don't have, so what's the point of reporting?" she replied with an attitude.

Deep down, I knew Andrea was right, but I just wanted his ass sooner than later. For some reason, I didn't think that it would take so long, but I guess I wouldn't tell all my secrets this soon either. Maybe I did need to lay off of Andrea and let her do her job. Her mouth had gotten much more mouther than usual. I couldn't lie. The way Andrea just put me in my place had me turned on. I knew I shouldn't be thinking about her like that, especially since I was fucking her best friend, but she had me hard as shit. I just hoped that she didn't look down.

"A'ight, Andrea. I'm sorry for speaking to you that way. You're right, I was out of line. Please forgive me."

"You're forgiven, but please don't speak to me like that ever again. And for now on, if you don't get a text or call from me, then that means I don't know anything worth talking about. But I do have a question. What are you going to do if he never let me in or discusses his business with me? And why is bringing him down so important to you? We've brought people down for less and know people that are doing more, so what it is about Mr. Santos?"

I sat quietly for a moment pondering if I should be honest with her or not.

"Honestly, Andrea, Javier killed my brother a few years ago, but it wasn't enough evidence to put him away for the murder, so I figured I would try another way," I told her, leaving out the part about him being a dead man the minute the gates close.

"Wow, Captain. I knew this shit was personal. I just wish you would had have told me that shit before putting me on the case. I gotta go," Andrea stated angrily before getting back in her car and peeling off, leaving me standing there looking dumb.

I truly hoped that me telling her the truth didn't fuck up the case I worked so hard to build, but the one thing that I knew about Andrea that was honest: she took her job seriously. I just hoped she continued to do her job and bring that bastard down. I was almost ready to just kill that nigga myself. I got back in my car and drove off. I had to go back to the office and make reservations for me and Jessica tonight. I wasn't sure where I wanted to take her yet, but I knew it was going to be someplace nice.

Chapter Eleven

Andrea

I had just got to Javier's club for Kye's surprise birthday party. I was rocking an all-white, off-the-shoulder, one-piece romper. The top part of the romper was lace. I wanted to be comfortable yet elegant and sexy. I wore a pair of silver rhinestone, open-toed, heeled sandals. It was funny because today was the first day of Spring, so the weather was perfect for what I had on. I had done something crazy with my hair, but I loved it. I had Shyanne dye it honey-blonde and shave the right side of my hair down. So, I had loose, honey-blonde curls going to the left side of my head, and on the shaved part, I had her put three lines with a sharp point. I couldn't wait for Javier to see me. Hell, I couldn't wait to see him and what he was going to be wearing.

Ever since the day he got shot in the warehouse, he and I have gotten pretty close. A little too close if you asked me. I had fallen for Javier in the worst way.

"Damn, girl, you looking good. My brother is going to die when he sees you," Shyanne stated with a wide smile, causing me to smile as well. "I'm really glad my brother met a woman like you. I've never seen him so happy before, so thanks for making him a better man," she said sincerely.

"Thanks. I love your brother," I stated honestly.

It felt good to say that to someone without being judged by them. I know I should have been happy to hear everything that Shyanne just said to me, but the truth was, I felt like shit. I knew that this love story would soon end, and I would lose a good man and a good friend. Because I could never be with Javier, even though I wanted to. I had to constantly remind myself that this was just work.

Shyanne was just about to say something else when I felt a pair of hands on my waist, and I knew that it had to be Javier. The smell of his cologne had me feeling some type of way down below. I turned around to face him and instantly became wet.

"You look stunning, baby," he complimented before kissing me on the lips.

"You're looking damn good, yourself," I said back.

Javier was wearing a royal blue, short-sleeve button-up shirt with a pair of white jeans and a pair of royal blue shoes. I wasn't sure how much longer I was going to be able to hold out from having sex with him. If he didn't make a move soon, I would. I knew that would only complicate things even more, but that was a risk I was willing to take.

******

The party was popping, and everyone seemed to be having a great time. The place was pretty packed, and there was security everywhere. The music was blasting, and everyone was on the dance floor, including Javier and Kye's parents. I was surprised to see them so loose because they were pretty uptight and kinda bougie, but not tonight. Shyanne and Kye had been acting a little weird all night, and now she was sitting in the corner holding a glass that was still full.

"Hey, sis. What's going on with you? You don't seem like yourself." Her eyes quickly filled with tears, and now I was curious about what the hell was going on. I'd never seen Shyanne cry before.

"I'm pregnant, Kamyra, and this baby has my hormones all over the place. I found out that I was pregnant two weeks ago," she cried.

"It's going to be okay, but who's the father? I've never seen you with a man," I asked curiously.

"It's Kye's baby, but please don't say anything to anyone, especially Javier. He doesn't know about us."

"Shyanne, when were you going to tell me that you were pregnant?" I heard a voice say, and when we looked up, it was Kye.

"I'll let you two talk," I told her before walking away. I didn't want any parts of that.

The party was finally over, and Javier asked me to come back to his place. I gladly agreed. As soon as we got in the house, I wasn't sure what had gotten into Javier, but he pushed me up against the wall and started kissing me wildly. Not being able to control myself, I kissed him back. I started undressing him. I ripped open his shirt, ripping all of his buttons off in the process. Javier picked me up and carried me to his private elevator that led to his room. My heart was beating loud enough for anyone to hear. I was excited and nervous at the same time. I hadn't been with a man in years—three years to be exact. And Javier would only be the second man that I'd ever been with.

Javier had now taken all of my clothes off, as well as his. We were now both standing here naked as the day we were born, taking each other's bodies in. I stared in disbelief at how blessed this man was. We started kissing again, and Javier placed kisses on every inch of my body. When he reached my center, he began to feast on my sweet nectar as if it was his last meal. For the rest of the night, Javier and I had the greatest sex that you could have. I had no idea that sex could feel like that. He did things to my body that I didn't even know was possible to do.

"Damn, Kamyra, you got some bomb ass pussy. It almost felt like I was your first," he joked, bringing me from my thoughts.

"Nah, you weren't my first, but you're only the second guy that I've been with, and I haven't had sex in three years," I told him honestly.

He looked at me like he was waiting for the joke to be over. "Wait, you're serious? Didn't you just have a boyfriend?"

"Yes, I'm serious, and yes I had a boyfriend but we weren't serious so we never did it and, no, I don't want to talk about it. But what I do want to do is go another round," I expressed while climbing on top of him.

For the rest of the night, Javier and I had sex until the sun rose.

Chapter Twelve

Kye

"How the hell can you sit here and be happy about me being pregnant? I can't have this baby, Kye," Shyanne stated.

She was starting to piss me off. If she thought for one second she was getting rid of my seed, she was crazy as hell.

"Look, Shyanne. I'm tired of arguing about this. You're not getting rid of my child, and I mean it. I don't want to talk about this anymore because it's starting to piss me off," I snapped.

I hated talking to her like that, but this shit was crazy. I didn't see what the big deal was. We've known one another our entire lives, and our parents were best friends.

"I think you need to leave, Kye, because I need some space," Shyanne said before storming off.

She and that hot ass temper of hers, and the mixture of hormones, had me ready to choke her ass. But I decided to leave before I said some shit that I couldn't take back. She was gonna be pissed at me tonight because our families were having dinner at my parents' house, and I planned on telling them. So, I would play nice for now, but tonight, that shit was coming out. Shyanne had me fucked up if she thought I was about to be treated like some side nigga.

The name is Kyree Jenkins, but my family and close friends called me Kye for short. My parents, Marco and Marie, have been together since high school. My dad and Javier's dad used to run the drug business together, but I never wanted any parts of it. I knew everything there was to know about it. I was a professional shooter and had no problem with killing a motherfucker, quick, if I had to. But I chose not to be in the game. It just wasn't for me. Instead, I decided to go into real estate. I owned one of the largest real estate companies in the world. I'm the one who got my parents, Javier, and Shyanne's houses for them. All of our houses weren't too far from one another.

I had just turned twenty-seven last week. I had two years on Javier and three on Shyanne.

*****

I'd just got to my parents' house. It'd been a little over a week since I'd seen them. I'd been so busy with work. I walked in and the food was smelling good. Marisol was my parents' cook and had been since I was a little boy. I found my parents in the family room, along with Uncle Franklin and Aunt Shanice.

"Hey, everyone," I said, hugging them each.

"Well, hello. I had to throw a dinner just to see my son," my mom said with a smile.

"Chill with all that, Mom. It's not even like that. I've been busy with work," I told her.

The doorbell rang, and I was sure it was either Javier or Shyanne. When I looked up, Shyanne, Javier, and Kamyra walked in. After everyone spoke, we sat down to eat dinner. Marisol had outdone herself this evening. We had steak, shrimp, chicken, and fish along with potatoes, mac and cheese, corn, asparagus, rolls, and a salad.

"Kamyra, you're glowing. You must have finally let my son hit that," Aunt Shanice said.

That shit was normal. I swear these people had no chill. Kamyra just smiled.

"They look good together," my father stated.

"Yes, they do," my mother chimed in. "Son, when do you plan on settling down instead of pussy hopping all the damn time?" she asked, causing Javier to laugh.

I thought now was the perfect time to tell them about me and Shyanne. I peered over at her, but she was too busy stuffing her face to see me looking.

"I'm glad that you asked because I already been seeing someone," I said, catching everyone's attention. Shyanne looked at me with pleading eyes, but she was just gonna have to be mad.

"Nigga, you ain't tell me that you met somebody," Javier blurted.

"I would have been said something, but she didn't want anyone to know, but now that she's pregnant, it's no reason to keep it a secret."

"You let some chick treat you like some side chick?" Javier joked

"Oh, my God, son. Who is this woman, and when do we get to meet her?" my mom quizzed.

"It's Shyanne. We've been dating for the last few months, she was scared to tell y'all. I wanted to tell y'all, but I also tried to respect her wishes. Yet her being pregnant changes everything," I told them honestly.

The room fell silent, and I could see the tears forming in Shyanne's eyes, but this needed to be done.

"Nigga, I know you didn't just say you fucking my sister and got her pregnant?" Javier said, getting up from the table.

I got up along with him because, best friend or not, I didn't play that being up in my face shit.

"Javier, you need to chill. Me and Shyanne are grown and don't need your permission!" I barked. I wasn't trying to beef with my bro, but he needed to tone that shit down before things got ugly.

"Nah, nigga! Your ass ain't good enough for my baby sister! You ain't nothing but a fucking dog! Not to mention, this shit is disrespectful as hell from both of you!" Javier yelled, now standing in my face.

Him telling me that I wasn't good enough for Shyanne had me in my bag, and him standing in my face like he wanted to fight me, with as close as we were, had me feeling some type of way.

"You need to get the fuck out of my face," I told him.

Our parents were telling us to calm down, but things were about to get too heated at this point to just walk away.

"Or what, nigga?" he asked, taking a step closer.

Before it knew it, I punched the shit out of Javier, causing him to stumble but not fall. He threw a punch back, and we fought it out until our fathers finally broke us apart.

"Have y'all niggas lost your fucking minds? Fighting like to niggas off the street in my fucking house and disrespecting these women! I'm disappointed in both of you! Y'all need to go!" my dad said angrily.

I just stormed out without saying another word. I needed to smoke immediately. I hopped in my car and peeled off.

When I got into the house, I poured myself a drink and lit a blunt. I couldn't believe that I'd just fought my best friend of damn near thirty years. That nigga had the nerve to tell me that I wasn't good enough for Shyanne. He was tripping with that one. Ever since the first night me and Shyanne hooked up, I hadn't fucked nobody but her. Yeah, I had my fair share of women, but I was also a single man. I had way too much respect for Shyanne to cheat on her or hurt her. I'd been in love with Shyanne for years, but I wasn't ready to give up my hoe days at the time.

But I'm grown as hell now and was ready to settle down. From the moment I slid up in Shyanne, I knew that I was going to marry her. I just didn't know it would be this soon. I was going to talk to Uncle Frank when this shit cooled down and ask for her hand in marriage. I couldn't allow her to bring a baby in this world without making her my wife first.

For the rest of the night, I just smoked and replayed the shit that happened at dinner over and over again. My phone was ringing nonstop, but I didn't feel like talking to anybody, so I powered it off, took a shower, then took my black ass to sleep. I was over today's events and would deal with this shit tomorrow.

Somebody constantly ringing my bell woke me up from my sleep. I knew it was family because nobody outside of my parents, Javier, and Shyanne had the code to get past the gate. I looked at the time, and it was in the morning on a Saturday. So now I was pissed. I jumped up and went to the door. Shyanne came storming in. It looked like she had been crying.

"Kye, how could you do that to me last night? I told you I wasn't ready to tell anyone, and now Javier is pissed at me," she cried.

"Shyanne, the shit needed to come out. I should have been said something. Because if I kept waiting on you, no one would have ever known. And you worried about Javier being mad, but do you even care how I feel or what I'm going through? I fought my best friend/my brother last night in my parents' home. They are going to chew a hole in my ass when I face them again. I don't see the big deal. And you need to calm down and stop all this stressing while you caring my baby."

I pulled Shyanne in for a hug, and she just laid her head on my chest and cried. I hated seeing her cry. That shit was doing something to me. I made a mental note to go holler at Javier later on.

"This is just a mess, Kye and I don't know how to fix it."

"It's nothing to fix. Everything's going to be okay," I assured her. "Now let's go lay down for a couple of hours. It's too early for all this dramatic shit."

"Kye, I can't lay down. I have clients in a few hours," she whispered.

"Nah, you don't need to go in today. Clear your schedule and spend the day with your man. Let me take you shopping and out to eat. I wanna spoil you today. But, first, I have a few houses to show. Once the clients leave, we can be nasty," I told her.

She looked at me and rolled her eyes before agreeing to what I said.

Chapter Thirteen

Andrea

Shit had been crazy over the past two weeks. I swear it seemed like as soon as me Javier started fucking, all hell started breaking loose. Between Javier tripping over Kye and Shyanne having a baby, down to his drug business, I didn't know what to say. Javier still hadn't told me much about his operation. Right now, I had enough on him to have him arrested. The problem was, I wasn't sure that I wanted to turn him in. The captain was pissed with me since I hadn't told him anything yet, and my best friend still had been acting strange. At this point, I wasn't even sure if we were still friends, let alone best friends. Shit was getting crazy, and I was in a very fucked up position. I was too far gone to turn back now. I was officially in love with the wrong side of the law.

"Hey, baby. You didn't hear me calling you?" Javier asked, startling me.

"I'm sorry. I was just in deep thought."

"What's on your mind?"

"I think that you're being too hard on Shyanne and Kye. I know you don't like talking about it, but I think it's time that we did. Those two have known one another their entire lives, just like you and Kye have. They love each other, Javier, and for you to act like they did something wrong isn't right. The three of you need to talk," I voiced.

"Look, I appreciate your input, but this is between me and my sister, and I don't want to talk about it," Javier said, dismissing me and my feelings.

I had to meet with the Captain in a few hours, but I decided to swing past Jessica's house first. When I got there, I could have sworn that was the Captain's car parked out front. *What the hell was he doing here*, I wondered. I use my key and tiptoed through the house. The closer I got to her door, the louder the moaning became. I put my hands over my mouth in disbelief at what I was hearing. I wondered when the hell did those two start fucking around. The noises came to a stop, and I was about to leave until I heard them talking.

"So, what are you going to do about Andrea?" Jessica *asked.*

I was curious about what she was talking about, so I put my ear closer to the door so I could hear a little better.

"Honestly, I don't know, she not riding with us anymore. We may have to kill both of them because I know she's holding back at this point. Andrea forgot that this is just a

job, and she went and fell in love that nigga. So we gonna have to do a bust and make sure that both of them die somehow."

"Trevor I can't kill my best friend. I know we not as close as we used to be, but she's still my best friend."

"Jessica, cut the shit. We both know that's not your best friend. She's barely a friend. You said it yourself that she was too in love with Javier to turn him in and that she needed to be dealt with. You also said that she had a new best friend. She doesn't know, but I've been following her, and I plan to have her house wired. It's time for this shit to come to an end. So, you in or what, Jessica? And just know that it's no turning back from this point forward."

"I'm in, but please don't make her suffer. Our plan has to be airtight and not come back to us."

They had me sick to my stomach. I couldn't believe they were planning to kill me. I ran out of the house like someone was chasing me, got in my car, and peeled off. I cried all the way to my house, and as soon as I got in, I found myself bent over the toilet throwing my life up. I was hurt and scared, and I had nobody in my corner besides the person I was sent to take down. And his sister, which I considered my best friend. I had nowhere to turn. The only way to keep my life was to run far away and leave behind the only family I seemed to have, just to get away from the family that thought I once had.

It was hours later, and I was still crying and throwing up. Once I got myself together, I packed a bag and headed to a hotel for a few days. I knew I was wrong for just up and leaving, but I needed some time and space to myself. I pulled up to the Ritz hotel in Philadelphia and checked in for a week. Once I got settled in, I ordered some room service because I was starving. I took a long, hot shower while I waited for my food to come. Once I got out the shower I dried off and threw on something comfortable. Soon after my shower was finished, my food arrived. I had ordered steak, potatoes, and green beans. After I ate, the only thing I wanted to do was sleep. I climbed into bed and stared at the ceiling until I fell asleep.

The next morning, I jumped up from my sleep and ran over to the bathroom. I barely made it to the toilet before I was throwing up everywhere. I didn't know what the fuck was going on. After cleaning my mess up, I powered on my phones, and I had a dozen missed calls and text messages from Javier, Shyanne, and some from the Captain, as well as a few from Jessica. I wanted to reach out and tell Javier that I was okay, but I couldn't face him or Shyanne. And as far as the Captain and Jessica go, they were out to kill me, so I needed a plan and quickly.

I powered my phone back off and decided to hang out in Philly for a few hours. I wanted to do some shopping and eat some good food. Once I had more bags than I could carry, I put my bags in the car, then drove to Ms. Tootsie's soul food restaurant. Once I was seated, I ordered some smothered turkey chops, baked macaroni and cheese, and some collard greens.

*****

It'd been four days, and last night was the first time that I responded to Javier and Shyanne. I just simply told them that I was good, and I would call them in a couple of days, then powered my phone back off. I knew Javier was going to be pissed, but I just couldn't face him right now. I felt like shit for what I was doing to him and his family. They would be torn to pieces if something happened to him. I mainly felt bad because Javier had been talking about going legit more and more.

He said that he had enough money to live a great life and support his family without ever hurting for any money. Plus, he wanted to open up a few more clubs and a few casinos. I didn't see a reason to take a man's freedom away for something he wasn't even planning to do anymore. A knock on my room door broke me from my thoughts. I figured it was housekeeping because I didn't order room service. I opened the door and was shocked to see a very angry Javier standing there.

"Javier, what are you doing here, and how did you find me?" I quizzed.

He walked in and shut the door before the tongue lashing started. "Kamyra, have you lost your fucking mind up and leaving like that and not answering my calls or text? I was worried fucking sick about you!"

For some reason, him yelling at me brought tears to my eyes, and I couldn't understand why the hell I was crying. "I'm sorry, Javier. I just needed some space from everything," I cried.

"Kamyra, I don't want to hear that crying shit. Why would you need space from me?"

I swear I wanted to tell him so badly, but I just didn't have the heart. So, I just cried even harder. Javier didn't say anything else. He just held me while I cried. I jumped up and ran to the bathroom to vomit. This was the third time this week that I'd thrown up. I guess I was stressed the hell out.

"Baby, get your shit and let's get out of here. And don't even think about telling me no," he said.

I didn't have the energy to argue, so I packed up my things and left with him. He didn't even let me drive my car. He said someone will come to pick it up later

The ride back to Javier's place was quiet, and my ass was in the passenger seat with tears rolling down my face. I had to find a way to escape because I couldn't turn him in, and my boss and so-called best friend were planning to take me out. I needed a plan, and I needed one quick. When we got in the house, Javier told me to go shower and he would be up soon. After my shower, I put something comfortable on and checked my messages and emails.

Shyanne: *Kamyra, where the hell are you? I hope you're okay. My brother over here tripping and shit. Please text or call one of two and let us know if you're good.*

Jessica: *Andrea, I need you to call me. I miss my best friend, and I've been calling and texting you for days. Not to mention, Cap is worried sick about you.*

For some reason, Jessica's text pissed me off, and I wondered what the hell was she up too. I would soon find out because I was going to pay her a friendly visit this week. I needed to act like she was still my friend and see if I could find out what she had up her sleeve. I was about to call Shyanne when Javier walked into the room. He was wearing a look that I wasn't familiar with.

He stood there and just stared at me for a minute before speaking. "That shit you pulled, Kamyra, was reckless and disrespectful. I was worried fucking sick about you. I don't give a damn what you got going on. You should have told me. I'm supposed to be your man, yet you can just bounce like I'm a nobody. I had to track you down, Kamyra, and I'm not too happy about that. What the hell do you have to say for yourself?"

His tone reminded me of my father's. He was talking to me like I was his child but in a somewhat scary but calm tone.

"Javier, I'm sorry for the way I up and left, but I was really going through something and just needed some space. I was going to call you, but I knew if I would have told you that I needed to clear my head, you would have talked me out of leaving for a few days, and I needed that time away," I told him honestly.

I mean, of course, I couldn't tell him that I'm an undercover cover cop that was sent to take him down, but since I'd fallen in love with him, I didn't want to turn him in. Not to mention, since I haven't turned him in, my boss and best friend are now out to kill me.

"That's' no excuse, Kamyra. I feel like something more is going on than what you are telling me. I'm going to leave it alone for now because the truth always comes to the light. Besides, we have more important shit to deal with than that little stunt you pulled."

I wondered what he meant by more important business to deal with. "I don't know what else to say but I'm sorry, and what do you mean we have more important business to deal with?" I asked curiously.

"Here, go take this," he said passing me a pregnancy test.

I looked at the test, then at him. I was confused as hell why he would be giving me a pregnancy test because there was no way in hell that I was pregnant. "Why the hell are you giving me this, Javier?"

"Kamyra, please just go in the bathroom and take the test. You running away and being suddenly emotional— plus, I've been hitting every day, and you haven't had a period since April fifth," he stated.

I thought about what he said, and Javier was right. I didn't get my period this month. I didn't say anything. I just took the test and walked to the bathroom.

I sat on the toilet sweating bullets because being pregnant was the last thing I needed right now. I peed on the stick, then wiped myself and stood up and washed my hands. Javier knocked on the door, and I let him in.

"So, what did it say?"

"I haven't looked at it yet. I just did it just before you knocked on the door," I told him.

Javier walked over to the sink, picked up the stick, and looked at it. A smile appeared on his face before handing me the test back. I looked down and damn near had a heart attack. I couldn't believe I got so caught up to the point that I allowed myself to get pregnant. The tears instantly rolled down my face, as I shook my head "no" as if someone asked me a question.

"Why are you crying, Kamyra? This is a beautiful thing," he said, touching my stomach.

"Javier, I can't have no baby right now. I'm just not ready for all of that," I cried.

"The hell if you can't have my baby. I know you don't think you getting no fucking abortion and killing my kid," Javier said angrily.

His voice scared me, and I knew he was going to be a big problem. I needed a plan. I was going to have to find a way to bring him down and get an abortion, or I was gonna have to run far away.

"Are you telling me that I don't have a say so on if I want a baby or not?"

"Kamyra, of course you have a say, as long as you're not saying that you're getting rid of my child. Let's just drop the subject for now and celebrate. We're going to be parents Kamyra," he said excitedly.

If this was under normal circumstances, I would be happy too. I always wanted a family of my own, but not by a kingpin that I was supposed to be setting up. However, I knew I wasn't gonna win this conversation, so I would just have to pretend until I thought of a plan.

"You're right, baby. This is a celebration. I guess I just got scared, that's all."

I wasn't lying about the scared part because I was shitting bricks right now. I'm surprised he didn't hear my heart beating out of my chest. For the rest of the day, me and Javier sat and talked, made love, and ate all kinds of food. I could get used to this, but it was too bad that it could never be.

Chapter Fourteen

Javier

I wasn't sure what the fuck was going on with the people in my life these past few weeks. I swear it seemed like I just couldn't catch a break. My sister was fucking my best friend behind my back, and now she's carrying that nigga's baby. Not to mention that Kamyra tried to run away for a few days without saying shit to me about it. I knew there were a lot of things that I kept in the dark from Kamyra because I wasn't fully ready to open up to her just yet. But the fact that she was now carrying my baby kinda changed some shit for me.

Something had been off with Kamyra, and I didn't feel like I could trust her. She'd been making sudden store runs and insisted to take herself. Not to mention the way she was shooting the night I got shot. That shit was only something that you saw on television or from a highly experienced person. I never said anything to her about it because I planned to do some more homework on her ass. Whenever I had a suspicion about something, I kept it to myself until I could prove it, then I'd bring it to your attention.

I was on my way over to my parents' house. They called themselves having a family meeting. I was sure it was about Kye and Shyanne's sneaky asses. I still wasn't fucking with any of them right now. I knew I wouldn't be mad forever, but I needed some time to process all of this.

My parents and Kamyra felt as though I was overreacting about the entire situation, but I didn't give two fucks about any of their thoughts. I felt betrayed and disrespected, and I doubted there was anything that could be said to change my mind. Especially if there is no sincere apology attached to it. For some reason, both of them acted as if they didn't understand what they did was wrong.

Depending on how things went tonight, I might tell them that Kamyra was pregnant. I wasn't sure if she had already told my sister since they were damn near best friends. When I pulled up to my parents' house, I instantly got pissed because I saw Kye's car parked in the driveway. When I walked in the house, they were in the family room. My parents, Kye's parents, and him and Shyanne was there laughing and joking.

"Well, hello son. Come have a seat," my mother said.

I walked over and gave my mom and my aunt Marie a hug, then dapped my dad and Uncle Marco. I looked over at Kye and Shyanne and gave them a head nod, then took my seat. I had just got there, and yet I was ready to leave. My dad walked over and handed me a drink, and that's just what the fuck I needed to help me get through this meeting.

"Javier, we called all of you over because we're sick of this feud that y'all have going on. And it needs to be dealt with and end today," my father stated. "I understand that you feel disrespected and Kye should have come to you as a man before fucking your sister because that's what men do. Especially if he's serious about her. But they are two grown adults that are about to bring a baby into this world. So whatever y'all need to do to squash this shit, y'all need to do it. If y'all need to fight it out, here are the boxing gloves so y'all can handle your business. But after tonight, I don't want to hear shit else about it. Do I make myself clear?"

"Clear," I answered back.

"Bro, I'm sorry for not coming to you first, but that shit just happened. I know this is no excuse, but I wanted to tell you the very next day. Yet Shyanne insisted that I didn't. We argued a few times over it because I wanted to tell all of y'all. I don't mean any ill when it comes to Shyanne. I've been in love with her since we were kids, and I do plan to do right by her and make her my wife," Kye had the nerve to say.

For some reason, him calling me bro got under my skin. "It's funny how you calling me, bro, but you're fucking my sister. Wouldn't that also make her your sister?" I said.

I knew I was probably being petty as fuck right about now, but I could care less. I was pissed, and that was the bottom line.

"Oh, I see you on that fuck boy shit. Maybe we need to fight this out because I'm sick of your fucking mouth and the blatant disrespect. I'm trying to be a man about this shit, but you making it real hard. You already know I love you, but if you keep this shit up, I'm gonna have to put these paws on you," Kye threatened.

I knew he was serious about fighting me, and I also knew that he would give me a run for my money. Deep down, us fighting probably wasn't necessary, but as men, our egos were too big to not do so.

"Is that right? I think maybe we do need to fight it out, then," I said, getting up and grabbing a pair of gloves.

I was over this shit. He hopped up and grabbed the other pair, and I knew there was no turning back.

"Are y'all serious? Y'all going to fight over this? This is stupid, and I will not sit around and watch my brother and my man fight over something so dumb. Kye, if you fight him, don't bother coming over tonight," Shyanne said, standing up to leave.

"Then I guess I'll see you tomorrow because I'm fighting his petty ass," Kye shot back. He walked to the back yard, and everyone followed, except Shyanne, until my mom made her come along.

We both put our gloves on and squared up. Kye was sick of my shit and threw the first punch. I blocked it, but that second punch connected with my jaw. I threw a combo: one shot to the face and the other to his chest. We yelled at one another to get some shit off our chests as we fought like two men off the streets. I swear it seemed like we were fighting forever until Uncle Marco broke it up.

I rested my hands on my knees and tried to catch my breath. This fighting shit was tiring. That's why it was easier to just shoot a motherfucker.

"I hope y'all little niggas got what you needed off your chests because this is the last time I want to hear about this shit. And Shyanne, this what happens when you play your brother and your best friend against one another. You had no right messing with Kye without speaking to your brother about it. Let this be a lesson," my dad said before walking back in the house.

I was on my way back in the house and Kye pulled me back.

"Yo', I am sorry about how I went about things. I missed the hell out of you," he stated.

"You good, bro. You know how my stubborn ass gets, but that was a good right hook."

We both just laughed because as long as we'd been friends, we'd never fought. I don't even think we argued before, to be honest.

"Your hands aren't too bad, either," he replied.

Me and Kye hugged that shit out before we went back in the house.

"Yo', I wanted to tell you first. You fitting to be a God daddy," I told him with a huge smile. I was happy about the pregnancy and couldn't wait to meet my bundle of joy. I knew for sure I was about to leave the streets much sooner than I expected.

"Oh, shit. You knocked baby girl up? Congrats, Javier. I'm happy for you. Well, I guess it's time for us to settle down and see what this family shit's about."

"I guess it is, and, Kye, congrats to your ass well. Please understand this the first time you hurt my sister, I'll kill you. She's not like those other females you been playing around with, so as long as you treat her right, you have my blessing," I told him seriously.

I didn't play about my sister. Shyanne was my heart, no matter what we go through. I'll kill for that one. When I walked in the house, she walked up to me and hugged me tightly.

"Javier, I'm sorry for not telling you. I didn't think you would be so pissed about it. But Mom and Dad talked to me, and I understand where I fucked up at. I love you, big bro," she said, placing a kiss on my cheek.

My sister could be a pain in my ass at times, but I loved her to death. I was going to tell them about the baby tonight, but I'll them another day when Kamyra was with me so we could do it together.

******

It'd been a few weeks since everything had popped off, and I was glad that shit was back to normal. Me and Kamyra were still somewhat on the outs. Shit just hadn't been right with her, so I hired a private detective to find out everything that he could, including where she'd beeb going when she left the house. If she and I were going to have a baby, I needed to know everything there was to know about her and her family. She didn't come off as a liar, but I still needed my facts.

I pulled up to my club because I needed to take off a few things before I headed down to Atlantic City for the weekend. I was about to open a casino, and I needed to tie up some loose ends. I hadn't decided if I was going to ask Kamyra to come with me or not yet. I might leave her at home so I can see what she was up too. Ever since I found out she was pregnant, shit had been seeming a little off. I couldn't help but wonder if her meeting Shyanne was coincident or intentional.

When I got to the club, I walked straight to my office and went through my business emails. I had a few emails that I needed to attend to right away and some that could wait. After replying to my emails, I placed in my food and liquor order before heading home. I texted my driver and told him to pick me up. I didn't feel like driving myself home. When I walked in the house, the aroma from the food that was cooking hit my nostrils and caused my stomach to growl. I walked into the kitchen to see what Ms. Claire had cooking. I was surprised to see Kamyra's sexy ass in the kitchen setting the table in a white one-piece lingerie set. At this point, I was ready to fuck and eat dinner later. I was ready for my dessert.

"Damn, baby, what you got going on in here?" I asked, wrapping my arms around her waist.

I inhaled her fragrance and kissed the back of her. She let out a soft moan. I turned Kamyra around, picked her thick ass up, and placed her on the kitchen aisle. I leaned in and kissed her lips softly, but after a few seconds, she stopped me by placing her finger over my lips. I was looking at her ass like she was crazy. A nigga was ready to let one off.

"No dessert before dinner. We gonna play a little game. If you can get through dinner without touching me, then I'll be your sex slave for an entire week—doing what you want, when you want, and how you want. However, if you don't make it, you owe me a vacation somewhere on an island for at least seven days, starting next week," Kamyra stated seductively.

I just closed my eyes and bit down on my bottom lip. There was no way in hell that I was going to make it through this dinner without sliding up in her. So, I might as well as book our flights.

Without replying with words, I dropped to my knees and started feasting on her sweet nectar. Kamyra had some good fucking pussy. That shit was always tight and wet. Since she'd been pregnant, that shit really been good as fuck. After having my way with Kamyra right there in the kitchen, we were finally able to eat dinner, and I must say, baby girl can throw down. She made one of my favorites: T-bone steak cooked medium-well, homemade garlic mashed potatoes, and green beans with honey biscuits. I was full and ready to shower then take my ass to sleep. After I showered, me and Kamyra's horny ass ended up fucking for a couple more hours before finally falling asleep.

It was now Friday, and we were on our way to her first doctor's appointment. A nigga was excited as hell. I was glad that her appointment was in the morning because I had to head down to Atlantic City at twelve. When we got to the appointment, I was glad that it wasn't packed in the waiting room. Kamyra signed in and filled out some paperwork while we waited. A few minutes later, a woman came to the door and called Kamyra' s name. We both got up and walked to the back. The nurse was eye-fucking me hard as hell. She better hope like hell that Kamyra didn't see that shit because her mouth had been out of pocket ever since she'd been pregnant. I wasn't sure if it were the hormones or what. After the girl took Kamyra's vitals, on her way out, she stared at me smiling.

"Excuse me, is something wrong with your eyes? I swear you hoes are disrespectful. You can leave now," Kamyra spat.

The girl was standing there looking dumb ass shit, but I thought the shit was funny as hell. "I'm so sorry. I wasn't trying to be disrespectful," she explained, but Kamyra just rolled her eyes at the girl. The girl hauled ass out that room.

"What's so damn funny, Javier?"

"I'm laughing at you. This jealousy thing is kinda cute."

"I'm not jealous. I just had to check her ass for being a disrespectful, thirsty hoe."

Before I could respond to her crazy ass, the doctor walked in.

"Hello, my name is Doctor Wallace. I'm going to need to perform a pap smear and get some lab work. I would also like to perform an ultrasound to see how far along you are and to make sure that the baby is measuring to where it is supposed to be. You can put this gown on and you can take everything off. I'll be back in a couple of minutes," he said before walking out the room.

Kamyra took her clothes off, and I swear it seemed like she developed a baby bump from nowhere. The fact that she was pregnant with my seed made her even sexier than usual. The doctor tapped on the door before walking in with an aid.

"Are you okay with him being in here while we perform the pap smear?"

I looked at him like he was fucking crazy. "With all due respect, of course I'm allowed in here. That is my baby she's carrying. Not to mention, if she didn't want me to be in here, she wouldn't have brought me. Besides, no man would ever be looking in my woman's pussy without me being present," I told him seriously.

"Sir, I didn't mean to offend you. It's just standard protocol to ask."

I didn't feel the need to reply, and I could tell that Kamyra was embarrassed by what I said. But I wasn't the type of man that sugar-coated anything. After he performed the pap smear, he started with the ultrasound.

"This may be a little cold," the doctor warned.

The joy that came over me when I saw my little bundle of joy on the monitor had a nigga ready to cry. I grabbed Kamyra's hand as I watched a tear fall from her eyes. I couldn't believe that I was about to be a father.

Chapter Fifteen

Andrea

It had been two days since I went to the doctor, and I was still overjoyed. I was unsure about how I felt about me being pregnant until I saw my little one on the monitor. I still wasn't sure what I was going to do, but what I did know was, I wasn't getting rid of my baby for anyone. I was sad that I couldn't tell the one person I could always talk to about anything that I was expecting. Javier's family seemed to be the only family that I had. And although they may have been truthful about their feelings for me, I was pretending to be something that I wasn't. My love was real for Javier, but I knew I couldn't be with him.

Javier had been gone for two days, but he'd be home this evening. I was missing him like crazy and couldn't wait to see him. This baby had my hormones raging. All I wanted to do was have sex day in and day out, and, of course, Javier was always with it.

I was on my way to meet up with the Captain to report and try to see what he had up his sleeve. I knew I shouldn't have met up with him, but I couldn't let him know that I overheard him plotting to kill me.

"Well, if it isn't, Ms. Andrea. Where the hell have you been?"

"Javier has been keeping a tight leash on me, so it's hard for me to get away. I keep telling that when I have something worth talking about, then I would call you like I did today."

"So, what do you have? Please tell me it's something big."

"Well, I know he has a big shipment coming in two weeks. It's supposed to be huge. I'm not sure where the pickup is at just yet, but I do know that it's about to go down. So, I figured once I know the place the shipment is going, you can bust him then," I lied.

Captain had a wide grin on his face like he'd won the lottery or something. I figured if I said in two weeks that would buy me some more time.

"That's good news. You were starting to scare me a little bit. Get me the info as soon as possible so I could set a plan in motion. Do you think you could convince him to let you go? That way, I can bust you along with him, and whoever else is involved, so shit doesn't look too suspicious. But, if not, you can just disappear and go back to your normal life without him ever even suspecting your involvement."

"I'll see, then let you know how I think we should proceed. I'm ready for this shit to over and done with so I can get back to my normal life. But whatever you do, please wait for me. I'm practically living at his place, so I can't afford any fuck ups. We're too close to get sloppy."

I was laying that shit on thick, and he was buying right into it. I hadn't seen him this happy in a while. I guess that I could breathe for a minute because if he thinks we're close to bringing Javier down and I'm still on the right team, he won't try to kill me for the next couple of weeks.

After meeting with the Captain, I decided to visit my dear friend, Jessica, but I had to run a few errands first. I had to pay my rent and bills for a real place of residence. Since Javier was out of town, I decided to ride past my house and check the mail. Although my life as Andrea was pretty boring and only consisted of work and home, I was kinda missing it.

I couldn't believe I got myself caught up to the point I had to take my baby and run and hide. I was so glad that I had money saved up to start a new life. I just had no idea where I would go. While driving up Jessica's block, I saw the Captain pulling off. I didn't use my key this time. I rang the bell. I had already told Jessica I was on my way. I had to be careful because she was an enemy, and I wouldn't be surprised if he had her house bugged. Neither of them could no longer be trusted, but I was gonna see if she would at least tell me about her and the Captain. I knocked on the door, and Jessica answered right away.

"Hey, best friend! I missed you so much. How's everything going?" she asked cheerfully.

"Everything is going pretty good," I told her. "So, what's new with you? Are you seeing anyone yet?"

"Girl, I wish. My life is boring, especially with you being gone."

"Well, if you not gonna get a man, you better go get some dick. It's not like you to sit around and like Virgin Mary."

"Drea, I haven't had dick in so long, but it's cool. I've just been chilling," that bitch said, lying through her teeth.

I just went with it. I sat and chilled for about a half hour more before heading to Javier's place. We were having dinner at his parents' place tonight so we could tell them about the baby.

*****

After my shower, I stood and looked at my naked body, and my pregnancy was very much visible. I rubbed on my small baby bump with a smile. I was only two months and had a long way to go. My phone buzzed, breaking me from my thoughts.

Javier: *I'm going to send a car for you in a half hour, and I'll meet you at my parents' house.*

Me: *Okay.*

By the time I was finishing getting dressed, the car was already outside. I got in the car and we pulled off. I was a little nervous to announce the pregnancy. I didn't want to get him or his family hopes up high, knowing damn well that after a few more weeks, they would never see me again. Let alone meet the baby. I was thinking about moving to the islands or something. Maybe I would try to find some of my mom's relatives.

We pulled up to Santos' house, and even though I'd been here a few times, at this point, I still couldn't get over how big and beautiful this place was. Or how it was just for two people. But I guess when you have the kind of money they have, these are the type of things you do with it. When I got out of the car, the door opened, and I was greeted by Javier. He seemed a little off, but I couldn't tell what was wrong. I went and spoke to everyone that was in attendance, which was Javier's and Kye's parents and Shyanne. After eating a wonderful dinner, Javier stood up to speak.

"Good evening, family. I called this family gathering to announced a few things. First, I will be opening up two of my casinos as of June, which is next month."

"Son, that is great news. I'm glad that you're branching out and opening up a few businesses of your own. Me and your mother are very proud of you," Javier's father stated.

"Yes, son. I knew you were destined to be great the day you were born. I love you, son," Javier's mom said.

Of course, the table started clapping and shit.

"Moving on, my next announcement is even bigger. Me and Ms. Kamyra White are expecting our first child," Javier announced. And everyone went wild with their congrats, I felt like shit sitting at the table knowing they would never meet this baby. "Wait there's more," he stated, now really grabbing my attention. I swear this man was full of surprises. "My next announcement is dedicated to Ms. Kamyra White, or should I call her Ms. Andrea Moore?"

My stomach dropped to the pit of my stomach. The table was confused about what he was saying and begin to ask questions, but I was too fucking scared to listen to what they were saying. Javier walked closer to me and grabbed me by my hair.

"Kamyra, why don't you explain to me and my family who the fuck you are," he said, grabbing my hair tighter.

The tears formed in my eyes. I wasn't sure exactly what all he knew, but what I did know was, he knew my real name, and that was a problem. As a matter of fact, let me tell them.

"This bitch is the worst of them all. She's a fucking cop, y'all," he said while shaking his head. Javier let out a psychotic laugh before drawing his gun me.

At this point, I was scared shitless. I had my gun on me, but this was his family, and his family's house, so my little gun wouldn't do shit for me right now.

"Javier, I'm sorry. I didn't want to do it, I swear I didn't. Please don't hurt me, Javier. I'll tell you everything, but don't hurt me," I pleaded.

My plea fell upon death's ears because Javier smacked me so fucking hard with the gun, I had blood leaking everywhere.

"Javier, have you lost your fucking mind? I understand that you're pissed, but she's still carrying your child!" Mr. Santos yelled.

I prayed that to God that me carrying his child still meant something. If not, I was as good as dead and would never even meet my little one. Shyanne was wearing a weird look on her face as walked towards me. "Dad's right. She's carrying your seed, bro. So don't kill her yet. Besides, she's a cop, so the plan has to be airtight. We can't have this shit traced back us, but trust me, she will get dealt with," she stated before her fist came crashing into my face.

All I could do was cry. I couldn't believe that my secret was out. I had no idea how much longer I would be alive. Javier asked for some tape and a blindfold. He then patted me down and took all my personal belongings like my phone, purse, and my bag.

Once Javier had what he needed, he handed the gun to Shyanne, and she held it on me while Javier tied my hands and placed a blindfold over my eyes.

"Javier please don't kill me. Just let me explain," I cried.

"Shut the fuck up!" he yelled, placing duct tape over my mouth.

I didn't want to die. I finally had a life worth living for. I was pregnant by the man of my dreams, and I wanted to be with Javier and raise my unborn. Now, me or the baby will live. Javier started walking me somewhere, but I was unsure where. All I could do was cry. I had fucked up in the worst way, and now there was no turning back.

I heard Javier on the phone telling someone to meet him at the spot, as we drove to god knows where. The ride to wherever we were going was quiet. The car finally came to a stop after driving for what seemed like forever. We started walking, and I heard keys followed by a door being unlocked. The door opened, and we walked in, then down a set of steps.

I felt my blindfold come off, and I just knew that I was gonna be in some gutter looking basement, but instead, I was in a space that was bigger than my apartment. I still had no clue to where I was. I just wanted to lay down. My head was pounding, my face was sore, and it was still leaking blood from being pistol-whipped and punched.

"I can't believe that you're a fucking cop and that you played my ass. From this moment forth, you're going to do exactly what I tell you, and you will answer any question that I want to know. Or I'll kill your ass," he threatened.

I just simply nodded my head.

"You look a mess, Andrea. First question: is that my baby?"

"Yes," I answered.

"Good, because that's the only thing keeping you alive right now. I'm going to cut to the point. I'm going to untie your hands and let you get cleaned up. This will be your new home until the baby comes. I already took everything that you own, and I'll have someone go over to your place and clear that out as well. First thing tomorrow, I'm getting a DNA test. You already played me once, but you won't do it again. This place will have around the clock security, so don't try no dumb shit unless you and the baby want to die."

Javier untied my hands. He then showed me the bathroom and where I would be sleeping.

"Javier, will you at least let me explain?" I mumbled.

"Nah, I'm good on the explanation. It ain't gonna be shit but a lie anyway, but if I feel like I need to know something, then I'll ask. Until then, don't say shit to me. I'll be back tomorrow. Now going get cleaned up," he stated harshly before exiting the room.

I heard locks being put on, and the tears rolled down my face. I walked around the place, and it was an apartment. I had a nice bedroom, a kitchen, a bathroom, and a decent size living room. I guess it was a good thing that I was pregnant with his baby or else I things would be a lot worse, and I would be dead.

Chapter Sixteen

Trevor

It'd been two fucking weeks since I heard from Andrea. I tried tracking her phone and still nothing. Something didn't feel right in my gut, and I wanted to make sure the girl wasn't dead. Jessica said she hadn't heard from her either. I knew I was about to take a risk, but if I didn't hear from her in a couple of days, then I was going to pay Javier a little visit, or send Jessica over. Andrea took her time giving me information, but it wasn't like her to be MIA. I went by her house, as well as the apartment I got for her, but never got an answer. The next time, I'm gonna kick the bitch in. I couldn't even locate her car.

"Trevor, something just doesn't seem right with Andrea disappearing like that. You don't think it's funny that as soon as she told you she had a lead that she just disappeared? What if he killed her or something, Trevor?" Jessica rambled.

I mean, she had a point, but I just didn't want to think the worst. I know I said I was going to kill her, but I don't think I could have gone through with it. I like Andrea a lot, and I'm really worried about her.

"Baby, I know. We gonna figure something out. Maybe you can go past the sister's hair shop, and tell her that you're her friend from out of town."

"Okay. I'll give it two more days, then I'll go by the shop. I don't know what I'll do if something happened to her."

"A'ight, baby. That sounds good. I have to get to work and so do you," I said, placing a kiss on her lips.

I was starting to fall hard for Jessica, although I didn't plan on it. But, hey? Shit happened. It was getting harder every day to keep us a secret.

When I got to work, I just couldn't keep still. I had to find Andrea. I sent over some undercovers to go pass both of Andrea's houses to see if anything looked suspicious, or if anyone was lurking around. If that punk ass nigga did something to Andrea, I was for sure going to kill him and everyone involved. I felt like shit for even putting her in that situation for my own selfish reasons, and if something happened to her on my watch, I could never forgive myself.

*****

A couple of days had passed and Jessica was on her way to the shop. I had her wear a wire and a body cam so I could hear everything that was going on. She should be pulling up any minute. I was parked not too far away from the hair shop in case some shit popped off. When Jessica walked in, I was impressed with the way the shop looked. It was upscale.

"Hi, I'm looking for Shyanne?" Jessica said to the receptionist.

The receptionist picked it up the phone and Shyanne's fine ass walked out.

"Hi, what can I do for you today?" Shyanne asked Jessica.

"Hi, my name is Jessica, and I'm a friend of Kamyra's. I have been calling her for weeks, and she's not answering. I live in Georgia, and it's not like her for us to not to talk. I figured I would come here since she told me how close you two were, and she also mentioned that she was dating your brother. Is my friend okay?"

"I'm sorry you came so far to see me, but I haven't heard from Kamyra, either. And, yes, we were close, and, yes, she was dating my brother, but not anymore. My brother came home to a letter stating that she was leaving town. She said something to the effect that she wasn't who he thought she was, and she had to leave town, and she was sorry for breaking his heart," Shyanne told Jessica.

"What did she mean by that? I don't know where she would go, if not back to Georgia with me. I'm the only family that she has besides you and your brother, Javier, right? I'm worried sick about her. If I don't find her, maybe I should go to the police. Did you mention a letter? Do you think your brother would let me get a copy of it?" Jessica asked.

I could tell that Jessica was taking this hard, and I couldn't blame her. They'd been friends for a long time.

"We're worried about her too. We have been trying to find her, but no luck. We didn't go to the police since she wrote a letter, which meant she left on her own free will. I'm sure he won't have a problem giving you a copy. You know her better than us, so if you think you should go to the cops, then that's what you should do. We can use all the help that we can get. We love Kamyra, and my brother is heartbroken beyond words. But if you can leave me your number, I'll call you about the letter. I'm sorry to end this conversation, but I have a client to attend to," Shyanne said dismissively.

Something still wasn't sitting right with what she said, but then, again maybe all of this was too much for Andrea. Maybe she did run away so she wouldn't have to turn Javier in and risk him finding out who she was. Jessica wrote her number down and headed out the door. I followed behind Jessica until we pulled up at her house. When she got out of the car, she looked like she had been crying while she was driving.

"Trevor, do you believe her? Do you think Andrea left town? This is all your fault, Trevor. You pushed her too far. She tried to back out when she felt like it was too deep for her, but you forced her to stay," Jessica cried, burying her face into my chest.

I couldn't say anything. I just held her because she was right. This was my fault.

"I don't, Jessica. I should have taken her off the case. I was being selfish, and now she's disappeared. Once we get the letter and see if it's her handwriting, we can go from there."

I stayed with Jessica longer than I should have so I could comfort her, but as soon as she fell asleep, I went back to work.

Later that night, Jessica came up to the station and barged into my office crying. She handed me a paper, yelling that it was Andrea's handwriting. I took the paper and looked at it. It was, indeed, Andrea's handwriting, but I still had to find her, and I still wasn't convinced that Javier didn't do anything to her.

Chapter Seventeen

Javier

It'd been three weeks since the private detective called me and told me that Kamyra was a fucking cop. I wanted to kill her on the spot, but she was carrying my seed. I had a DNA test performed, and it turned out it that it was my baby. I had a doctor that came out to check on her once a week. She and the baby were doing good. I hadn't seen her since the day I dropped her off, but I'm going to visit her later today. I'd been keeping my distance. One, so I wouldn't hurt her, but the biggest reason was that no matter how angry and hurt I was with her, I was also still in love with her. Kamyra, or should I say, Andrea, had my heart in the worst way. I had never felt like this about anyone one before.

Shyanne called me and told me about her so-called best friend showing up to the shop asking questions, but I'm sure she was probably a cop as well. I knew they would come sniffing around. That's why I had her write a letter so they could have her handwriting and think that she left on her own.

I had to go past my parents' house before I went to Andrea. Ever since I learned her real name, I couldn't pull myself to call her Kamyra. I walked into my parent's house and didn't see anyone.

"Aye, Pops, where you at?!" I called out.

"I'm in here, son!" he yelled.

I walked into my father's office and he was pouring himself two drinks.

"Hey, Pops. What's up?"

"Hey, son. Have a seat," he said, passing me a drink.

Whenever my father called me over and poured a drink, that meant he wanted to talk about some heavy shit, and I wasn't sure if I could handle anything else on my plate. I had enough shit going on. Between my baby mom being a cop and trying to open up my casinos, I was fucked up mentally.

"Listen, I know you're going to do what you want, but as your father, I have some shit I think you need to hear."

"Come on, Dad. Just say what needs to be said. I have to run a few errands," I said impatiently.

"Boy, don't' rush me. I know that tactic you trying to pull. But let me get to the point so you can go run your errands. I think you're wrong about Kamyra."

Hearing him mention her name caused me to give him my full attention. "What you mean, Dad?"

"Son, you only get one true love, and I can tell that Andrea is it for you. I can also tell you that you're hers. I know she's a cop and came to you under false pretenses, but that doesn't mean she didn't fall in love. She's carrying your first child, Javier. And you know how we are about family. I know you're gonna raise that baby as a single man because you want to kill the mother of your child for doing her job. Sometimes, we all have to do shit that we don't want to do to pay the bills. But that girl is in love, and you at least owe it to her to hear her side of the story. I know you, and you're probably thinking you would be a fool to still be with her, but I disagree. I think you would be a fool to let her go so easily."

"Dad, how the hell could I trust her after learning this shit?"

"Ask yourself this question, Javier. Has she betrayed you since y'all been together? If she told them anything, how come you still on the streets?"

His questions made me really think about what he was asking. Like I thought when I first walked in, this was gonna be some heavy shit that I wasn't prepared to deal with right now. I just shook my head before downning my drink. I needed some air and quick.

"Thanks for the talk, Sad, and I'll take everything that you said into consideration. But for now, I have to go. This shit is too much to deal with right now," I stated before making my out the door.

*****

I ended up having to make a run to Atlantic City to sign some paperwork for my casinos I was about to open in a few weeks. I'd just pulled up to the spot I had Andrea stashed, but I wasn't sure if I was ready to see her just yet. When I walked into the house, I unlocked the door, and Andrea was in the kitchen cooking something to eat. She was beautiful in every way. She looked up at me and stared at me like she had seen a ghost. Although I was angry and hurt, I hated to see her sad.

"Hi," she mumbled above a whisper.

"Hi," I spoke back.

"I didn't think I would see you again," she stated sadly.

"I wasn't ready to see you. Finding out that you're a cop and you came to take me down broke a nigga's heart. I was serious about you, Andrea, and to make matters worse, you're carrying my first seed. I'm not gonna lie. If you weren't, I would have killed you. That's how disrespected I felt."

Tears filled her eyes, and I knew I shouldn't have cared about her feelings, but I did. Maybe my dad was right. Maybe I should listen to her side and go from there.

"Javier, I know, and I'm sorry. I didn't want to do it. Well, at first, I was cool because it was my job, and I didn't know you. But as soon as I got to know you, I asked to be taken off the case, but my boss refused. I even told him that this was bad because I was falling for you. I swear, Javier, my feelings for you are real. My boss was upset with me because I wouldn't give him anything on you. To be honest, I didn't have much to give at first, but even when I learned a few things, I just didn't say anything."

I was about to cut her off, but she stopped me.

"Please let me finish. Now that's it's all out, I need you to know everything. I did plan to leave in a couple of weeks because I didn't know what to do. I couldn't tell you I was a cop, and to make matters worse, I overheard my boss and my supposed to befriend plotting to kill me. All because they felt like I wasn't gonna give you up because I was in love. They have no idea that I heard them. The same day that you got back from AC, I made up a story and told him I had something that would bring you down, and that it was a big shipment coming in a couple of weeks. He was so happy and so was I because I knew it would buy me some time to get away," she cried.

My gut told me she was telling the truth. So maybe she was on my side and wouldn't turn on me. Nothing else was said. Nothing was heard besides the sniffles from Andrea. I just held her as she cried. I wanted to kick myself for caring about her so much.

"Javier, I love you," Andrea stated.

I didn't say it back. Instead, I bent down and kissed her lips. That one kiss led to a passionate night of loving making.

*****

The next morning when I woke up, Andrea wasn't in the bed with me, and I knew I had fucked up. How could I be so stupid and get caught up in the moment? Now I was for sure that she had escaped. Moments later, Andrea walked in the room carrying food. I was relieved and confused at the same time. She could have tried to escape not that she would have made it that far due to my security team. But the keys were in my pants pocket, and I was knocked out cold.

Before I could say anything, I heard the door and voices. I figured it had to be my sister. *Shit. She's gonna know I stayed here last night,* I thought to myself.

"Andrea, where are you?"

"I'm coming now," Andrea answered before leaving out of the room. I wasn't about to be hiding in my shit, so I walked out behind her.

"Javier, what the hell are you doing here?" Shyanne quizzed.

"That's not important," I told her.

"I know you didn't fuck her?"

I didn't bother to answer her question.

"Hello, Mr. Santos. Will you be here for the ultrasound?" Dr. Jackson asked.

"Yes, I'll be here. When will we be able to find out what we're having?"

"Since Ms. Moore will be four months in a few days, we may be able to find out today. I can't make any promises, but it is possible."

A smile crept on my face at the possibility of knowing whether I was going to be blessed with a son or a daughter. I stood on one side of Andrea and Shyanne was on the other side. I knew she was just as happy about the baby as I was, being as though this was her first niece or nephew.

The doctor started the ultrasound, and I got excited seeing my little munchkin on the screen. She turned up the monitor so we could hear the baby's heartbeat, and my heart melted.

"Well everything is looking good. The baby looks great and is growing how it is supposed to be. Now, let's see if we can see if we're having a boy or a girl."

I grabbed Andrea's hand and she squeezed it tightly. I noticed Shyanne's eye roll, but I would deal with her later.

"Alrighty, it looks like you're having a little princess," the doctor stated.

I swear I could feel the tears form in my eyes, making me feel like some kind of bitch. But I didn't care. I was having a daughter, and I knew now, more than ever before, that I had to leave this street shit alone. There was no way in hell that I was bringing my baby into this drug shit. Once the doctor was finished, she told us that she would be back next month for another set of labs.

"Congrats, bro. I'm happy for you," Shyanne stated sarcastically.

I knew I was gonna have to check her ass, but I didn't want to do it in front of Andrea. "Shyanne, I need to speak with you for a minute."

She rolled her eyes. She was lucky she was pregnant because I probably would've slapped her ass. We walked to another part of the house, and I locked the door just in case Andrea decided to pull something. As soon as we were alone, my sister and her smart-ass mouth got to running.

"Javier, you went through all of this just to keep fucking her?"

"First off, Shyanne, what I do with my dick is my business, but I'm not gonna take your disrespect and sarcasm. That shit stops today. Yes, I came over here and talked to the mother of my child and slipped up. Yeah, I'm hurt about how shit went down, but she is carrying my daughter, and to be honest, I'm in love. I hate that I can't stop the feeling, but I am. Dad called me over last night, and he thinks that I'm making a mistake by treating her like shit before hearing her out. So I heard her out, and I believe her, but now, I just have to figure out how to handle all of this shit. Her people already on it, so I don't know how this shit is going to play out. I'll probably need you, but I'll hit you up when I do."

"Bro, daddy is probably right. Kamyra, well, I mean, Andrea, is cool as shit, but I'm still hurt my damn self that the whole thing was a setup. I feel used, Javier. You know that I don't fuck with a bunch of females, but she and I hit it off good. I wanted to stay mad at her myself, but it's hard. We talked a few times, and her story does seem believable. I mean, what could she do? She had a job to do just like the rest of us," she said, shrugging up her shoulders sounding just like my dad.

I knew Shyanne would understand, but I wasn't sure about how my mom and was going to feel, and I already knew Kye was gonna have some slick shit to say. But I think I was going to see where this shit was going to go with me and Andrea.

"Thanks for being someone I can always talk to and for always having my back. I love you, Shyanne. You don't have to come here when the doctor comes. I'll make it my business to be here. I think I'm gonna see where things go with me and Andrea, but first, we need to come up with a plan to get the cops off my ass."

"Yeah, agreed. Well, call me later. I have to go meet Kye for lunch." Shyanne placed a kiss on my cheek before walking off.

I walked her to her car, then I took a deep breath before going back into the house with Andrea.

"So, we're having a girl," Andrea said with a smile plastered on her face.

"Hell yeah, and I can't wait to give her the world, and you," I mumbled.

She looked up at me with wide eyes. "Wait, you're not gonna kill me after I have the baby?"

"Nah. I love you too much for that, but, Andrea, you better not play me. We need to come up with a plan to keep your cop friends off my ass and yours." I stayed at the house and talked to Andrea for a couple more hours before leaving her.

Chapter Eighteen

Andrea

It'd been a little over a month since all the shit went down with me and Javier at his parents house. Although I wasn't living bad down where he had me, I needed some air and wanted to see daylight. I was tired of being cooped up in the house all day, every day. Surprisingly, things seemed to be back to normal between Javier, Shyanne, and myself. But we were still trying to figure out a way to fake my death so the captain and Jessica would be off my ass, and I wouldn't have to turn in Javier or worry about dying. But nothing that made sense came to mind.

I was waiting for Javier to come by. I had a special night planned for us. I cooked a nice dinner and planned to make sweet love to him until the sun came up.

"Drea, where you at?" I heard Javier calling me by the nickname he's been calling me for the past couple of weeks.

"I'm in here, baby!" I yelled from the kitchen.

"Damn, baby, it's smelling good up in here. What you got going on?" he asked.

"Just cooking my man some dinner. Then I was hoping we could have a little fun in the bedroom," I answered in a flirty tone.

"I like the sound of that, and that's all your horny ass think about is getting some of this dick," he shot back, causing me to giggle.

After eating dinner, I showered while Javier cleaned the kitchen. When I got out of the shower, I walked past the mirror and my baby bump seemed to have grown overnight. I rubbed my belly, and I thought I was tripping when I thought I felt my princess kick, but I wasn't because she kicked again. I was so excited that I let out a loud scream, and I guess I scared Javier because he came running to the bedroom like something was wrong.

"Drea, what's wrong?"

"The baby just kicked for the first time!"

"Are you serious?" he asked excitedly while rubbing my stomach.

"Yes, I'm serious. She did it twice."

Javier bent down and started talking to my stomach. This was something that he'd been doing since he'd been coming back around. He said he wanted her to know who he was before she was even born.

"Hey, daddy's little princess. You in here kicking mommy? Kick for daddy," he said to my stomach.

She kicked harder than she did the first two times, as if she understood what he was saying. The biggest smile appeared on his face, which caused me to smile. I truly loved this man with everything in me, and there was no way I was going to go a day without him. Javier led me over to the bed and started feasting on my sweet nectar as if it was his last meal. Javier and I made love into the wee hours morning. Once we were finished, we laid there in the dark and just talked. I laid my head on his chest and he just played in my hair.

"Drea, marry me," Javier stated.

I was glad it was dark so he couldn't see how wide my mouth dropped open in disbelief. I wasn't sure if he was serious or just caught in the moment. Either way, my heart was beating out of my chest, and I was speechless. I swallowed the lump that had formed in my throat before saying, "Javier, are you being serious?"

"I'm dead ass, Drea. I don't want to go another day without you being Mrs. Santos. I'll go get you a ring tomorrow."

A wave of joy overtook my body. I rolled on top of Javier and hugged him tightly while placing kissing all over his body. Of course, that led to me slowly stroking my future husband's love pole until we both climaxed and clasped on the bed and fell asleep.

*****

The next morning when I woke up, Javier wasn't in bed with me, and I wondered where he disappeared too. I still didn't have access to a phone, so I couldn't call him. I decided to take a shower and wait for him to get back. As the water cascaded down my body, I thought about Javier asking me to marry him. I was caught up in the moment last night, but how could I marry him? I was a cop and he was the kingpin. How the hell would that ever work? I was in one hell of a situation, and I had no idea how to fix it.

When I got out the shower, I lotioned down and tried to find something to wear. Not that I was going anywhere, but I still had to put something on. I made a mental note to let Javier know that I needed more clothes than I could fit. I smiled at the thought because I never saw the day that I would be a mother and a wife.

I don't know why I was thinking about this now, but thoughts of how the hell Javier found out that I was a cop came about. If he was in AC like he said he was, then how the hell did my clothes get here to this place? I had just left his place and everything was good. I wanted to ask him but decided against it. At least for now. A couple of hours later, Javier made his way back. When he walked in the door, he was holding some flowers.

"Hey, baby. I was starting to get worried," I voiced.

"I'm sorry. I just didn't want to wake you, but I had a few things that I needed to do. Here. I brought these for you," he said, handing me the flowers he was holding.

I took the flowers and smelled them. They smelled so good; I wasn't sure what kind they were, since I wasn't familiar with the different types of flowers. I sat them down, and when I turned around, Javier was on one knee. Even though I had already agreed to be his wife last night, for some reason, this felt different. It felt more real this time. My heart was beating fast and hard.

"Andrea Moore, from the moment I laid eyes on you, I knew there was something different about you. The chemistry we share is hard to deny. I love you, Andrea. Will you do the honors of being my wife?"

The tears fell freely from my eyes as I nodded my head yes. "Yes, I'll marry you, Javier," I cried.

He stood up and I hugged him tightly then kissed his lips. I couldn't have been happier.

Chapter Nineteen

Trevor

Ever since I got the letter that Andrea was supposed to have written, I'd been trying to find her even more. It was something that wasn't adding up. I had been following Javier, but he hadn't been anywhere but his home, to his parents' house, and he made a few trips to Atlantic City to a couple of casinos. My gut told me that she didn't just up and leave, but the evidence was saying that she did. No one felt like I had a case since she, indeed, had written the letter. I checked for fingerprints and they were hers. It all would have made more sense if he went to a stash spot or something, but nothing. Just his home.

I couldn't get a warrant to go inside of his home since there was no evidence. I knew she wasn't just hiding out in the house without ever coming out of the house. The same people since the day I started my surveillance were the only ones that went to the house.

Jessica had taken some personal time off. She just said that it was too much for her to handle. I guess I didn't make the situation any better. I had pretty much made her choose between me and her best friend. I even tried to have her help me kill Andrea. I was starting to feel like a fucked up individual going down the wrong path. A few times, the thought of Jessica tipping off Andrea about me killing her came to mind, but I quickly dismissed the thought. This shit with Andrea was fucking with Jessica in the worst way.

I pulled up to the station, grabbed my belongings out of the car, and went into the building. Everyone was looking all crazy, so I knew something had to be going on.

"What the hell is going on?" I asked.

"I'm what's going on?" I heard a familiar voice say.

When I turned around, my eyes were met with Andrea. I damn near dropped my shit that I was holding.

"Andrea, I was worried sick about you! Are you okay?"

"I'm fine, Trevor. I just came to give you these," she said, handing me some papers.

I looked down at her signed resignation, already signed by the Chief of Police.

"I just wanted to give you these in person," she stated.

"Andrea, what the hell are you doing? How could you do this in the middle of a big case?"

"For this reason exactly. You don't care about anyone but yourself. I've been standing here for less than five minutes after being missing for damn near two months, and your first thought is why did I do this to you during a big case? You're unbelievable," she said. She was on her way out the door when Jessica walked in.

Jessica looked like she'd just saw a ghost. "Andrea, I'm so glad that you're okay. I missed you so much!" she said excitedly, hugging Andrea tightly.

My blood was boiling so bad that rage had taken completely over my body. I made a vow that Andrea was going to pay for that stunt that she pulled. I couldn't believe that bitch went over my head.

"Jessica, I was just about to come to see you. Can you walk me out?"

Jessica just nodded as they walked out the door together.

"I need to see you in your office, right now!" the Chief yelled like I was his fucking child. If he was here, I knew this wasn't good.

"Chief, what are you doing here?"

"As of today, you are currently on suspension without pay until further notice. You are now under investigation. You can clear out your desk. This could take a while. Oh, yeah. Stay the hell away from Andrea Moore. If you go anywhere near her, I will have your badge and have you arrested."

"What the fuck is this about?! What did she tell you?!" I yelled.

"Lower your fucking voice. The FBI will be in touch."

I ran my hand through my hair and started packing my shit up. I was going to kill that bitch, so she better count her days because they were numbered.

"And I meant what I said about Andrea," he warned.

I didn't bother to say shit else because I was over it. I couldn't believe this shit was happening. I packed up all of my shit and headed out the door but not before knocking some shit over like I was a little ass kid with an attitude. When I got outside, I looked around for Jessica and that backstabbing bitch, but neither of them was nowhere to be found. When I got the car, I called Jessica's phone, but she sent me to voicemail three times in a row. I just got even more pissed, so I rode to Jessica's house, but she wasn't home.

Where the fuck is she? Is she the one who set me up? Because why was she even at the station? I thought to myself.

I just sat in my car and banged on the steering wheel. I know the chief told me to stay away from Andrea, but I called her number anyway, and the number was disconnected. I couldn't believe this shit. What the fuck was going on?

Chapter Twenty

Shyanne

"Ms. Santos, how are you doing this morning?" Dr. Lewis asked when she walked into the room.

"I'm good. I'm just excited about finding out what I'm having," I told her while squeezing Kye's hand.

Kye looked over and smiled at me. He wanted a boy, but I kinda wanted a little girl. However, if I didn't get a girl, I would be okay because I would have a niece that I could treat as my daughter. Andrea was only a month behind me, so our kids would grow up together and be close in age. This was my second ultrasound because the first time, the baby's legs were closed. So I was praying that they were open today. The doctor started the ultrasound, and my baby appeared on the screen. It made my heart melt. Looking at my baby and hearing the heartbeat always made me get teary-eyed. I was an emotional wreck with this pregnancy.

"Well, let's find out what we're having. Okay, it looks like we're having a little boy and a little girl," the doctor stated, stopping me in my tracks.

"I'm sorry, did you say a boy and a girl?" Kye asked, taking the words right out of my mouth.

I wasn't ready for two babies, so I hoped that she was mistaking.

"Yes, you have two of them in here. I'm not sure why this didn't show up earlier than now. But now, we have to do extra testing, so this visit may take a little longer than I attended for it to be."

My head was hurting, and I felt like I was dreaming. There was no way I was prepared to raise two babies. I was still trying to get used to the idea of having one.

"I'm kind of excited, but how did this happen?" Kye said to the doctor.

I wasn't excited at all. Shocked would be a better choice of words.

"Honestly, I'm not sure why I didn't see the other baby until now. She may have been hiding behind the other baby, but this isn't uncommon. I just need to run a few extra tests to make sure everything is okay with the second baby."

I just wanted this visit to be over because this was too much for me right now. The doctor performed a few tests and told us she would call with the results. When we left the doctor's office, Kye and I went to got something to eat.

"So, we having twins, huh?" Kye said breaking the silence.

"I'm not going to lie, Kye, I'm not ready for two babies. Now I have to worry about the second baby being okay. And how did I get pregnant with twins? Do twins run in your family? Because they don't run in my family."

"Babe, I'm not sure, but this is a blessing. Can't you see that? I know it's not what we were expecting, but it's not like we can't afford it. We both have more than enough money we could ever need to take care of a football team if we wanted to have one."

"Yeah, but I don't want that many kids. This is probably it for me," I told Kye honestly.

All I wanted to do was take a nap.

*****

I woke up from my nap and realized I was running late. We were having dinner at Javier's house tonight. I had to hurry up and throw something on and head out before Javier chewed my ass up for being late. He hated late people. The one thing I could say about my brother was, he was a very punctual person.

After getting dressed, I headed out the door and headed to my brother's place. I was glad that we didn't live too far from one another. When I got there, everyone was already present. Tonight was the night that I would announce the gender of the babies. I couldn't wait for the look on my parents' faces when they found out that I'm having two babies.

"It's nice of you to finally join us, little sister."

"I'm sorry I'm late, everyone. My nap just went into overtime," I told them, causing everyone to laugh.

"You good, sis. Now let's eat," Javier stated.

We all ate and talked for the first hour.

"I have some news to announce," I started. "We found out what we're having today."

"Oh my God, Shyanne. I didn't know that you had an appointment today. So what is my grandbaby gonna be?" my mom asked excitedly.

"Well, we're having a boy."

"Oh, this is great. You're giving me a grandson, and my son is giving me a granddaughter. I can't wait to meet my grandchildren," my mother said.

"Well, then you'll be even happier to know that I'll also be giving you a granddaughter because we're having twins," I said.

"Damn, sis. I'm happy for you. So I'm going to have a niece and a nephew to spoil? I can't wait. Well, not to take away from your news, but I also have an important announcement to make. I proposed to Andrea, and she said, yes. So we're getting married," Javier announced.

The entire table got quiet.

"Javier you can't be serious. She's a fucking cop. I told you not to kill her because she was carrying your child, but I didn't say marry the trader!" my mom yelled.

I knew this was about to get ugly, and I honestly didn't want to be here for it. I had my own shit going on, and I didn't feel like dealing with this.

I couldn't lie. At first, I was mad as hell at Andrea and wanted to kill her ass, but I understood where she was coming from. She had a job to do, and she did what she had to do, but Javier marrying her, especially right now, was a bit much if you asked me.

"Mom, please don't start. What is your problem with me marrying Andrea? I love her and she loves me. Not to mention the fact that she's about to have my baby. Besides, what makes her a trader, Mom, since you know so much? Who did she trade on besides herself? She resigned from being an officer for me—for our family. So, like I said, I'm marrying Andrea next month no matter who likes it or not. You'll either be there or you won't, but one way or another, it's going to happen!" Javier stated angrily.

Andrea was alright with me, and if my brother wanted to marry her, then he had my blessing. I don't know many people that would be willing to turn in their badge for a drug dealer that she was supposed to lock up.

"Congrats, bro and Andrea. I'm happy for y'all. I think you two should do whatever makes you happy. Besides, I need some great Godparent's for these twins," I said, trying to lighten the mood.

"Thanks, Shyanne. I would be honored to be your twins' Godmother," Andrea finally spoke. "Mr. And Mrs. Santos, I know you may not trust me, and I don't blame you, but I love your son with everything in me. I gave up my badge to be with him. All I wanted to do as a child was to be an officer of the law until the day I met Javier. I gave up everything to be with a kingpin. Some shit that y'all got him into at a young age.

"If I was a snitch or a bad person, I could have taken all of you down, but I didn't. But I'm going to say this and then I'm done. I'm not going to break my back trying to prove my love and trust for Javier to y'all. Javier and our unborn child are the only things that matter to me. Now if y'all would excuse me, I'm finished here," Andrea said, getting up from the table and walking off.

"Thanks, sis. I appreciate your blessing, unlike your bougie ass mother's. Y'all can show yourselves the way out, "Javier said, getting up from the table and following behind Andrea.

I knew my mom wasn't happy about this because that's just how she was. Plus, she wasn't used to anyone speaking to her that way, but Andrea had proven from day one that she wasn't the one to take shit from her. I knew deep down my mother liked Andrea, but she'll never admit it. My mom needed to understand that Javier was a grown man and was gonna do what he wanted regardless of anybody else's opinion.

Shortly after, me and Kye said our goodbyes and took our assess home. I'd had enough for one day.

Chapter Twenty-One

Andrea

Today was the day I was about to become Mrs. Santos. Today was a sweet and bitter day for me. I was getting married, and I didn't have any family or friends of my own to watch me walk down the aisle. I wished Jessica could've been here, but I knew she wouldn't show up. I lost my best friend because I choose to resign as an officer of the law. I just couldn't do it anymore. I was ready to live a normal life. I agreed to marry Javier and give up my badge if he went one hundred percent legit, and he agreed. So here I was about to marry the man of my dreams.

I wasn't sure if Javier's mom was going to show up. Shit hadn't been going too good with them since he announced that we were getting married, and that was a little over a month ago. Me and Shyanne were working on our friendship again, and everything was going pretty well. I was glad that everything was starting to fall in place. A few weeks ago, I heard that Trevor was about to do some Fed time. He'd been doing some illegal shit, not to mention he only wanted Javier to be arrested so he could have him killed. The guy that was supposed to kill Javier ratted to get out of the prison early.

We were having something small at a nearby beach, then taking our honeymoon in Bora Bora.

"Hey, sis. Are you ready to get dressed?" Shyanne asked, breaking me from my thoughts.

"Yes, I'm ready, and, Shyanne, thanks for being my Maid of Honor."

"No thanks needed. I'm just glad that I won't be the only one wobbling down the aisle," she joked.

"Tell me about it. I told him to wait until after the baby was born, but he didn't want to bring his daughter in the world without us being married. So, I said fuck it, why not? I just wished my father was here to give me away."

"I know this is hard, but take a look on the bright side. You have gained a father-in-law. He's not like my mom, and he likes you very much. Honestly, my mom likes you too. She's just too stubborn to admit it," she said with a smile.

We heard someone clear their throat, and when we turned around, it was Mrs. Santos.

"Oh, hey, Mother," Shyanne spoke.

"Hello, daughter. Could you give me a minute with Andrea, please?"

Shyanne just nodded and left the room.

"Hello, Mrs. Santos. I'm surprised to you here."

"Listen, I know I've been a bitch, but I just wanted you to know that I do like you for my son. You're good for him. Javier loves you, and that's all that matters. To be honest, you remind me a lot of myself. And I'm truly sorry for giving you a hard time. I'll be honored to have you for a daughter-in-law," she said while hugging me.

Again, I was surprised but I was happy.

The ceremony was about to start, and I was nervous as shit. I swear it felt like I was sweating bullets. The song started to play, and Shyanne walked down the aisle first. The wedding was simple: no flower girl, no ring barrier, and no bridesmaids. It was just Javier, Kye, Shyanne, and me. Sweet and simple. It was finally my turn to walk down the aisle. As I was walking, I spotted Jessica, and my heart just skipped and beat. I smiled and stopped because I wanted to hug her. We hugged in the middle of the aisle, and I could feel the tears falling from my face. I prayed this was a new beginning.

"I missed you so much, Andrea. I love you," she said into my ear.

"I missed you too, girl, and you already know how much I love you," I whispered back.

Jessica sat back in her seat, and I proceeded down the aisle. I was finally standing in front of Javier, and he was looking so good in his custom-made white tux. Our colors were royal blue and white. Javier reached in and kissed me. Yeah, I know we were a little out of order, but it was our wedding, and we could do what we wanted. As soon as we finished saying our vows, and I was finally Mrs. Santos, loud gunshots rang out, causing me to let out a scream. I had no idea where the shots were coming from, but I was scared. I wished the shots would stop, but they continued. My wedding had turned into a shootout. And I didn't have a gun to shoot back.

I locked eyes with my old Captain, Trevor, before I watched bullets hit my husband in the chest. Javier fell back and I screamed.

"Nooo!" I yelled running over to Javier.

He was bloody, and all I could do was hold my husband and scream for help.

Trevor was yelling out things that I couldn't make out. Before I knew it, Jessica was putting bullets through Trevor's body. My wedding had turned into bloodshed. Before I knew it, everything went black.

*****

I woke up in the hospital hooked up to machines beeping. I looked over and Jessica was sleeping in a chair at my bed side, but I didn't see anyone else. My mind had a flashed back to my wedding, and I started to panic and call out for Javier. Jessica jumped up and ran over to my side.

"Andrea, calm down. This isn't good for the baby," she stated.

"Where's Javier?" I cried.

"Andrea, please calm down first. I don't know how much you remember, but Javier and his mother were shot. Javier's not doing too good, and your mother-in-law didn't make it," she stated sadly.

I thought my heart stopped beating, but I was still breathing, so I knew I was still alive. My heart was hurting bad, and I needed to see my husband immediately. The machine started beeping, and the doctor came in.

"Mrs. Santos, I need you to calm down. The baby is in distress, and if we don't get this under control, we're gonna have to deliver the baby early," the doctor told me.

This was too much for me right now. It felt like my chest was tightening up, and I was starting to have shortness of breath.

"I just want my husband," I cried.

The doctor finally got my vitals and blood pressure down, but I was still crying nonstop. I was trying to be as calm as possible because I didn't want them to deliver my baby early. I was only six months pregnant. Besides, I couldn't have my daughter without Javier. I prayed my husband didn't die. I hadn't even been married for twenty-four hours yet. A few moments later, Shyanne walked into my room, and her face was red with dry tear stains.

"Hey, I see that you're awake now. How's my niece?"

"They said she's distressed, and if that doesn't change, they're gonna have to deliver her early. Where's my husband?"

"It's not looking too good, sis. He's in a coma, and my mom died. Andrea, my mother is dead," she cried.

All I could do was cry along with her. All of this was a mess, and I couldn't help but believe that this was all my fault.

"I'm gonna come back a little later to check on you, but I have to check on my dad. He's distraught. And, Jessica, I know I don't know you, but thanks for killing that bastard."

I was confused at first, but then it hit me that I saw her shoot Trevor. I had no idea that she killed him, though. I knew she had to be hurting because that was also his lover but, I would wait for her to tell me.

*****

I'd just got to the hospital. I was here visiting Javier like I'd been doing for an entire month. His situation was still the same. He was still in a coma. His father tried to wait for him to come out of the coma before having the funeral, but they couldn't wait any longer to bury her. I felt so bad for Mr. Santos. Shyanne had the twins two weeks ago, and I was due any day. I just prayed that my husband didn't miss the birth of our daughter.

I was sitting at my husband's bedside rubbing his head when the door opened. I looked up and it was the doctor.

"Good morning, Mrs. Santos. Can we talk in private for a moment?" the doctor asked.

I got up and walked with the doctor out of the room and into a conference room.

"I'm not going to hold any punches with you. We don't believe that your husband is going to come out of this coma. He's lost to much blood and has been a coma for a little over of a month now. We see these types of cases all the time, and people rarely survives these type of injuries. We think it may be best if you considered taking him off of life support and putting him in comfort care. If you need to call family up, you can do so," the doctor stated.

I knew this bitch wasn't asking me what I think he was asking me.

"With all due respect, doctor, but as long as there is even a one percent chance of my husband living, I'm not taking him off," I told her before getting up and walking back in the room with my husband. I sat back down and grabbed Javier's hand. I rubbed it gently.

"Hey, baby. I'm not sure if you can hear me or not, but if you can, I need you to listen to me. The doctors don't think you're going to pull through, but I believe you will. Javier, our daughter needs you. I need you. I'm due any day now, and I don't want to deliver her without you. Please, baby, I need you to wake up. I miss you and need you more now than ever, and you're gonna need me. Javier, please, baby just wake up. I want to look in your eyes and kiss your lips," I cried.

I didn't even realize that I was crying so hard until someone walked in the room, I looked up and it was the nurse.

"Mrs. Santos, are you okay?" she asked.

"I just want my husband," I cried.

She passed me some tissues then left back out of the room.

I sat there for about another hour just talking and crying to Javier. I even prayed with him with the hopes that he could hear me. I finally got myself together, and I was now ready to eat. I stood up to leave, and I could've sworn I felt Javier squeeze my hand. I looked down and his eyes were still closed, so I knew I was tripping.

"Don't leave," I heard Javier mumble.

I looked down and his eyes were fluttering, and the machines started to beep.

"Oh my God, Javier, you're awake!" I cried.

The nurses came rushing in, and once they saw that Javier was awake, they called for the doctors. I couldn't believe that my husband was finally awake. All I could do was cry.

"Mrs. Santos, we have to take your husband down for some test, but as soon as we are finished, the doctor will come out to get you."

As much as I didn't want to leave my husband, I felt like this would be a great time to give his family some good news. As soon as I left the room, I called Shyanne.

"Hey, sis. Is everything okay?"

"Everything is great. Javier is awake," I cried into the phone.

"Oh my God, I'm on my way," Shyanne said, hanging up the phone in my ear.

Forty-five minutes later, Shyanne, Kye, and Mr. Santos filled the waiting room. I told everyone exactly what happened word for word. We were still waiting to hear from the doctors. I was starting to get grow impatient. I went over a month without my husband, and now that he was awake, I still had to be without him.

I just prayed to God that he would be in the same bill of health, or better, once he fully recovered. I also knew that today was going to be a bittersweet day. I knew he was going to ask for his mom, and how could we tell him that she was killed at the wedding, and we already buried her because he was in a coma for over a month? About an hour later, the doctor finally came out.

"The family of Santos?" the doctor said.

I wobbled over to the doctor as fast as I could. "I'm his wife. How's my husband?"

"Your husband is still awake but is still a bit delirious and uncertain about a few things. But this is normal for what he has experienced. We expect him to make a full recovery. I'm waiting on one more test that we performed on his brain, and that will determine what life is going to be like for Mr. Santos."

"What do you mean it will determine what type of life he will live? Are you saying that my husband may not live a normal life?"

"These types of injuries are always touch and go. He's been in a coma for over a month. I can't guarantee anything, but I promise we will do everything that we can.

"I just want to see my husband."

"We normally only let two people in at a time, but under the circumstances, all of you can go back. Just please don't stay too long. He's going to need plenty of rest."

I walked to the back to see my husband. When we got to Javier's room, a nurse was taking his vitals. I found myself crying yet once again. That seemed like all I did this entire pregnancy.

"Hey, baby. I missed you so much. I need you to get well soon so you can be in the delivery room."

Javier just smiled and rubbed my stomach. Our daughter starting moving around wildly, as if she knew who was rubbing her. Everyone said their hellos followed by crying. I think everyone was just happy he was alive.

"Where's Mom?" Javier asked.

The entire room fell silent, and I knew this moment was about to get sad.

Mr. Santos stepped up to the bedside and just looked at Javier with so much sadness in his eyes. "Son, there's no easy way for me to say this, but your mother died…she didn't recover from her gunshot womb," he stated sadly.

Javier had a look of confusion as tears filled his eyes. "Dad, what are you talking about Mom is dead? Tell me you're lying. Go get my mom!" Javier yelled.

"Bro, she's gone, and we tried to wait for you to pull through, but they couldn't hold the body any longer. We buried her already," Shyanne cried.

As long as I'd been on this earth, I had never seen or heard a man cry the way Javier cried for his mother. It broke my heart to pieces to watch him endure so much pain. Kye walked up and hugged his best friend long and hard. The nurse came in and told us that visiting hours were over two hours ago, and we needed to come back tomorrow because Javier needed to rest to get better.

I knew I wasn't leaving my husband's side. I felt like he needed me now more than ever before, and I just couldn't leave him alone. After everyone said their goodbyes, I walked everyone out to the waiting room.

"Andrea, thanks for being there for my son. He's gonna need you. He made a great choice marrying you," my father-in-law said while hugging me.

"Thanks, Mr. Santos. I love your son very much," I told him honestly.

"I know you do, and call me Pops."

"Javier is lucky to have a father like you. Again, thanks for everything, Pops."

When I walked back in the room, Javier was laying in the bed staring at the ceiling.

"Hey, baby. I know everything seems like a lot right now, but I promise you we will get through this," I told Javier while placing a kiss on his lips.

"I can't believe my mother is dead, and I didn't even have a chance to attend the funeral. I'm gonna kill the mutherfucker that did this to us."

"Baby, he's already dead. I just want us to move on and raise our baby."

"When is my Princess due to arrive? It feels like I've lost so much time."

"I'm due any day now. I just really hope that you're out of the hospital before I deliver the baby. I don't wanna go through this alone."

"You won't be alone. I promise as long as I have a breath in my body, I will be in that delivery room no matter what," Javier promised.

Nothing else was said. I just laid my head gently on his chest and silently cried.

*****

It'd been two days since Javier woke from his coma, and he was coming along pretty good. The doctor told us this morning that Javier was expected to make a full recovery. The swelling in his brain had gone down, which was a good sign. They wanted to keep Javier for another night just for observation, and if everything went well, he would be able to come home sometime tomorrow. I was glad to hear that because I just wanted to sleep peacefully in my bed. I'd been up here every day, all day. I spent most of my nights here for the past month. The doctors tried to get me to go home numerous times, but there was no way I was leaving my husband.

I sat in the recliner watching as he slept peacefully. This had been something that I'd been doing over the past month. I needed to go home and shower so I could get back up here, but I didn't wanna wake him, so I would just wait until he's awake before I leave. I heard the door opening. When I looked over, Kye was walking in.

"Hey, sis. How are you?"

"I'm good. Just need to shower, but I didn't wanna leave him alone."

"Well, I'll be here for a minute, so if you wanna leave you can. But how's he holding up?"

"As you can imagine, he's taking it very hard. I'm trying to be here for him as much as I can while giving him space at the same time."

"Yeah, I can only imagine what he's going through. My nigga strong, he'll pull through."

"Yeah, he will. Let me get going and let you have some alone time. When he wakes up, tell him I went to get dressed, but I'll be right back.

As soon as I got in the house, I what in the room to find something to wear. Once I was satisfied with my outfit, I stripped out of my clothes and jumped in the shower. As I was washing up, I started feeling my stomach tightening up. The pain hit me out of now where. I grabbed my stomach and the shower bar so that I wouldn't fall. I could hardly finish washing up. That's how much pain I was in. I assumed that I was experiencing contractions, which were now coming at least five minutes apart. I quickly washed my private parts and slowly made my way back to the room.

"Ahh!" I screeched in pain.

I hit the intercom to call for Ms. Claire. I knew I was gonna need help getting dressed with all the pain I was in, but she was gonna have to call the ambulance or drive me to the hospital herself.

"Hello, Andrea. Is everything ok?"

"No, I think I'm in labor. I need you to come to help me."

When Claire walked in, she immediately started helping me get dressed.

"Baby, just stay calm. I'm going to help you put your clothes on and call the ambulance."

I was finally dressed, and as soon as I stood up, my water broke. "Oh my God I need to get to the hospital. I can't deliver my baby here in this house."

I was panicking, and I was in pain, which wasn't a great combination. The ambulance had finally arrived, and I was glad because I wasn't sure how much more of this pain I could take. I wished I could just reach between my legs and pull the baby out myself.

They placed me on the stretcher and told me to calm down. Their asses must don't have kids because how the hell could anyone be calm with all this pain I was in? I tried my breathing techniques, but that shit wasn't working. I just wanted drugs, and I wanted them now.

"Ms. Claire, can you please call Shyanne and let her know that I'm in labor?"

Ms. Claire did as I asked. I loved Ms. Clair; we had grown pretty close since Javier was in the hospital. She rode in the ambulance, and I swear it seemed like this was the longest ride ever. We were finally at the hospital, then it hit me that, even though Javier was awake, he was still going to miss the birth of our daughter. All of this was just too much to handle.

They took me straight to the back and got me hooked up to the machine and checked to see how dilated I was. The nurse said that I was six centimeters dilated. That wasn't good enough for me because I knew you had to be ten centimeters before you could push, and I was ready to push. I was happy to see Shyanne walk in the room. I knew she could keep me calm. Plus, she just gave birth a few weeks ago.

"Oh my God, sissy. I can't believe it's time," she said with a smile.

"It hurts so bad. I just want my husband," I cried.

"I know, Andrea. I know it wot to be the same because I'm not Javier, but I swear I'll be here every step of the way."

She was right; it wasn't the same, but Shyanne would just have to do. I could no longer take the pain. I was acting a fool and I knew it. I knew this was going to be my first and last child because I never wanted to feel pain like this again. They had finally given me the epidural, but I was still somewhat in pain. Eventually, they gave me some meds to keep me calm until it was time to push. I was so drugged at this point, that I could hardly keep my eyes open.

Chapter Twenty-Two

Javier

I laid there in the hospital bed thinking about my mom. I felt like I was living in a dream. How the hell could one minute, I'm standing at the altar marrying the woman of my dreams, to waking up out of a coma and finding out my mom was dead and already buried? I swear my soul was crushed beyond words. The only thing that's honestly giving me hope was meeting my baby girl. I've been married for a little of a month, yet I haven't reaped the benefits of being married. I knew this had to be hard for Andrea as well.

Kye was up here keeping me company until she got back from freshening up. Andrea's stomach had gotten so much bigger and looked like she was going to pop.

When I saw Shyanne for the first time, it was so much shit going on that I didn't even realize that she wasn't pregnant anymore. I had all types of shit on my mind. What about my businesses and a drug empire? Even though I was giving up the drug business, I still had some shit that I needed to finalize.

It'd been almost two hours and Andrea still hadn't made it back. Someone needed to check on her. My thoughts were cut short when Kye walked into the room. He had a weird look on his face.

"Kye, you good?"

"Yes, I'm good, but when Andrea left to get dressed, her water broke. So she's here on the maternity floor about to give birth soon."

"Oh my God, I have to go be with my wife. Call the nurse," I said excitedly.

"Bro, slow down. I'll call the nurse, but you know they're probably not gonna let you out this bed."

I wasn't paying his ass any mind. I made a promise to my wife, and I was going to honor it. I could not allow Andrea to bring my daughter into this without me being there to support her.

"Is everything alright, Mr. Santos?"

"Nah, my wife is about to give birth, and I need to be with her."

"Congrats, Mr. Santos, but I'm afraid that won't be possible. I can't take you up there; you're still a patient."

"Look, I don't give a damn what you're talking. I'm going to see my wife give birth. Now you can take me, or I will discharge myself and go up on my own. But one way or another, I'm going," I told her honestly.

"With all due respect, nurse, your might as well take him up there because if you don't, he's still going to go. He's been through enough. The man lost an entire month of his life. Are you gonna make him miss the birth of his firstborn?" Kye said on my behalf.

"Against my better judgment, I'm going to talk to my supervisor. I'm sure you're going to do what you want, but at least do it with precautions," she stated.

Ten minutes later, I was being pushed in a wheelchair to the labor and delivery floor.

"It's time to push, Mrs. Santos," I heard one of the doctors say as I was entering the room.

"Ahh, this hurts! I just want my husband," Andrea cried.

"I'm here, baby. I'm here," I said, catching her attention.

She looked up with tears in her eyes and mouthed the words thank you. I just nodded my head and try to help her get through this pain as much as I could. I was in love with the fact that in just a few short minutes, Andrea would be delivering my firstborn, but I hated to see her in so much pain. A couple of minutes later, I heard the cries of my princess. My nurse wheeled me closer to the bed so I could cut the umbilical cord. I couldn't even explain the joy that took over my body. Before I knew it, I was crying and didn't care who saw. The doctor placed the baby in Andrea's arms. This was one of the happiest moments of my life.

*****

It felt so good to finally be home and sleep in my bed without worrying about nurses and doctor's being in and out of my room every fifteen minutes. I was sitting in the nursery feeding my princess while Andrea was taking a shower. We decided to name her Blessing Alay Santos. Alay was an Indian name that meant a gift from God. I walked into the room to grab my phone, and Andrea was getting dressed. I immediately had a hard-on. I haven't had any pussy in forever, and I was ready to feel the inside of wife.

I wasn't sure if I could wait another four more weeks to make love to my wife. It'd only been two weeks since she had the baby, but I was attached like she had been here for years. My daughter was truly a blessing, and I truly wished my mom was alive to meet her granddaughter. I still hadn't had the chance to grieve my mother with everything that has been going. I knew when I finally did break down that it was going to be bad. Thinking about my mom made me want to go visit her grave and check on my dad. I couldn't imagine how he was feeling.

I pulled up to my parents' place and walked straight over to my mother's grave. My dad decided to bury her on their property, and I thought it was a great idea. Reading my mom's name on a tombstone fucked my head up. I couldn't believe my mother was dead and not from natural causes but because she was shot. I cried and talked to my mother for damn near two hours. I don't think I talked to her for this long at a time when she was alive.

"Mom, I miss you so much, and this shit is killing me inside. I'm trying to be strong for Pops and Shyanne, but a nigga is hurting, and I don't know how much longer I can keep this 'I'm so strong' act up. I missed your funeral because I was in a coma my damn self. I just got out a couple of weeks ago. But guess what? I'm a father now, and it's the best feeling in the world. I promise to be the best father I can be. Also, I decided to give up the drug business so I can focus on being a great husband and father. I'm about to go check on Pops then head home to my wife and daughter. I love you, Mom."

Chapter Twenty-Three

Jessica

The last few months of my life have been hell. I had gotten myself into something way too deep. I should have never started fucking around with Trevor. He was bad news all the way around. Once I started dealing with him, I pretty much fucked up a great relationship with my best friend. Me and Andrea had been best friends for years now. She was honestly the only person that I had until Trevor came along. I'd been messing with Trevor for about six months. I thought we had something real, but I don't think that was the case at all.

I'm starting to feel like he used me just like he was doing Andrea. I'd only spoken to Andrea a few times since her wedding. I wanted to warn her that her problems weren't over, but I was afraid to say anything. I didn't have anyone to protect me, especially knowing how crazy Trevor was. How do you explain a suspended officer of the law shooting up at an ex-officer's wedding and ended up killing someone? I couldn't believe that I had to be the one to shoot my lover and my boss.

The name is Jessica Rivera, and I was born and raised in Camden, NJ. I moved from foster home to foster home after my father killed my mother, and then himself, when I was just ten-years-old. I never had many friends or family members that I was cool with. Andrea was the first person that I connected with. I met her in the police academy, and we hit it off immediately. We'd been friends ever since. That's why all of this was so hard for me. At times, I wished that I would die. I had to find a way to get out of this situation without losing my life.

"Jessica, what's taking you so long with dinner?" Trevor asked, breaking me from my thoughts.

Yes, you heard right. Trevor was alive. He faked his death. That was his plan from the start. I was supposed to make up with Andrea and attend her wedding so when he started shooting, I could "kill him," and he could kill Andrea and Javier when they least expected.

"Trevor, relax. I'm making the plates now."

"Look, we need to talk. I'm planning on moving in on my plan in the next two months. It's time for you and Andrea to become best friends again. I don't wanna make any mistakes. I want both of them dead"

"Trevor, what about her baby? She just had her. Is it really necessary to kill them? You can't be that bad of a person. Who is supposed to take care of their newborn if you kill both the parents?" I asked honestly.

"When the fuck did you become so worried about them? Whose side are you on? I don't care who takes care of the baby! That's not our concern!" he yelled.

"Trevor, all I'm saying is, Andrea doesn't have any family to take the baby if something happens to her. Not to mention, what if we get caught? Who's going to take care of our baby?" I slipped up and said. The room fell silent for a moment and Trevor just looked at me for a second before speaking.

"Jessica, what did you just say? What baby? "

"Trevor I'm sorry. I didn't mean for it to come out like this. I just found out that I was pregnant a few days ago. I was waiting for the right time to tell you."

The look in Trevor's eyes scared me. I had no idea what he was going to do. He just laughed like a mad man and said, "Jessica I'm not ready for no baby. You need to make an appointment for an abortion first thing tomorrow morning."

"Trevor I'm not having an abortion. I'm having this baby rather you like it or not," I told him honestly. I didn't believe in abortions, so I knew that if I ever got pregnant that I was going to keep the baby.

"You not having this fucking baby!" he yelled.

I wasn't expecting what happened next. Trevor smacked me so hard, and out of reflex, I hit his ass back, but that was a mistake. Trevor balded up his fist and punched me repeatedly. I tried to fight back as much as I could. I needed to protect me and my baby. But the more I fought back, the more he whooped my ass. So I finally just stopped and took the hits. When he finally stopped hitting me, I had blood dripping from my mouth, my side was sore, and he even kicked me in my stomach a few times. I couldn't believe that he just beat me like I was a man on the streets.

For the rest of the night, I didn't say shit to Trevor. I stayed out of his way and tried to get the swelling on my lip to go down. I was surprised that my eye wasn't black and swollen with the way he must be in my ass. I knew I had to come up with a plan, and quick. If not, Trevor was going to kill my Puerto Rican ass. I hoped like hell, I didn't have any broken ribs, but I swear it felt like I couldn't move. I didn't know What my next move was going to be, but what I did know was, this couldn't ever happen again.

"Jessica, I'm sorry for putting my hands on you. I don't know what got into me, but I meant what I said about you not having a baby. We're not ready for all that right now, Jessica. We have plenty of time to have a baby after we handle what we need to handle with Andrea and Javier.

Then we can move away somewhere and start fresh. Hell, we could even get married, but now is not the time," Trevor said seriously.

He had to be out of his damn mind if he thought I was gonna marry him. I was about to get so far away from his ass. I just had to figure out how to do it, but for tonight, I decided to play nice and agree with him.

"Okay, Trevor. Apology accepted. Just promise you won't ever hit me again. And first thing tomorrow morning, I'll go down to the clinic. I need to handle this as soon as possible to be healed in time," I told him, lying my ass off.

"That's my baby, and, Jessica, I don't want to put my hands on you, but I hope like hell you don't ever force me to hit you again."

That statement alone let me know that he would, indeed, hit me again, and that was a no for me. I swear I thought about blowing that bastard's head clear off his shoulders when he went to sleep. He had me all the way fucked up. I went in the bathroom and into the medicine cabinet. I needed to take some pain pills immediately. After the whooping he put on me, I could barely even move. I hardly got any sleep because all I could do was silently cry and try to think of a plan that could get me out of this situation.

The next morning when I woke up, Trevor was still asleep. My body was still sore but felt a little better than it did last night. I laid my clothes out on the bed then went and took a shower. When I got out the shower, Trevor was sitting up on the side of the bed.

"And where the hell do you think you're going?" he asked.

"Trevor, we talked about this last night. I'm going to the abortion clinic."

"Damn, I forgot just that quick. Jessica, I'm telling you now. Don't try to pull no fast one on me. You better come back in here with proof of abortion or an appointment of one."

"Trust me, Trevor after the ass whooping that you gave me last night, I'll be getting an abortion," I replied sarcastically.

Once I was finished getting dressed, I headed out the door. I did go to the clinic so I can make an appointment just to have something to show his ass. Once I left the clinic, against my better judgment, I called Andrea. It was time that I told her everything.

"Hello" Andrea answered the phone on the first ring.

"Andrea, it's me, Jessica. I know it's been a little minute since you've heard from me, but I need you and Javier to meet me today as soon as possible."

"Jessica, is everything okay?" she asked in a concerned tone.

"Not really. It's really important, but I need to talk to both of y'all."

"Jessica you're starting to scare me."

"Andrea can you please just give me a place to meet you and Javier?" I heard her yell in the background, but I couldn't make out what she was saying.

"Ok, we'll meet you. I'll send you the address to the location."

As soon as we hung up, my phone beeped, indicating that I had a text message. I looked at the text, and it was Andrea sending me the address to a football field. I hopped in my car peeled off. As soon as I got to the park, I sent a text message to Andrea letting her know that I had arrived. In less than five minutes later she and Javier pulled up beside me. The three of us got out of our cars and walked over to the empty bleachers.

"Jessica, what's up, and what the hell happened to your face?"

I swallowed a lump that had formed in my throat. There was no easy way for me to tell her what I was about to tell her, but I had to do it.

"Andrea, I don't know how to tell you this, but Trevor isn't dead.

"What the fuck you mean he isn't dead?!" Javier yelled, scaring the hell out of me.

"Jessica, slow down. How do you know this?" Andrea asked.

"I know because it was all part of the plan. He had me come to your wedding so when he tried to kill Javier. After shooting him to fake his death, he wanted to catch y'all off guard and kill both of you. I'm so sorry, Andrea, but Trevor made me do it. And to answer your question, he's what happened to my face. He's been beating the shit out of me, and I'm scared. He wants me to get close to you so he can kill you and Javier.

"But I just can't do it. I don't have anyone else to turn to. You're the only family that I have, and I'm sorry for everything. You know I would never betray you if I wasn't being forced. The only way to stop Trevor is to kill him. I never thought I'd see the day where I'll say those words out of my mouth. I'm not the one to kill people. I'm an officer of the fucking law for crying out loud," I cried.

Andrea punched the hell out of me, catching me completely off guard. My face was already hurting and swollen, and then I was hit again. I knew this was a bad idea coming here.

"How could you betray me like this, Jessica? You were like my sister?"

"I just told you he's forcing me; do you think I wanna hurt you? I got my ass beat last night for defending you. Not to mention that I'm pregnant, and I'm scared he's going to kill all of us if we don't do something about it. I know you have no reason to trust me, but I need you to trust me if we're going to live," I cried.

Andrea was about to hit me again until Javier stopped her. "Baby chill out. She just said she was pregnant. I know she's not the most trustworthy person, but for some reason, I believe her."

"Javier, I wanna believe her too, but I'm so fucking hurt right now. This girl was like my sister. The only one that I ever banged with, then she betrayed me for a piece of dick," Andrea had the nerve to say.

"With all due respect, Andrea, didn't you do the same thing? If you ask me, what you did was worse. You traded on your entire dream. All you ever wanted to do was become a police officer, and you gave it all up for a kingpin that you were supposed to arrest. Now, suddenly, you don't understand how someone could fall in love and then change. I'm not using what you did for an excuse, but I need you to understand that this was never my plan. When I first started sleeping with Trevor, I thought that we had something good.

"That's until I realized that he was just using me the same way he was using you. I may have been blind then, but now, my eyes are wide open and I'm trying to help. I don't know if we could ever be friends again. I would hope that we could, but even if we can't, we need to work together on this and get rid of Trevor for good. After Trevor is dead, if you no longer wanna have anything to do with me, I understand. I'll move away you'll never hear from me again," I told her honestly.

"A'ight, I'm going to trust you this one last time, but I swear on my daughter, you bet not be on no bull shit, or I'll kill you myself," she threatened.

"And if you cross me, I won't hesitate to kill your pregnant ass," Javier threatened.

The way he said it sent chills through my body. I was so glad that I wasn't on no bullshit.

"Where does he think you are right now?" Andrea asked.

"He thinks I went to make an appointment for an abortion, which I did. I needed some paperwork to show him."

"When is your appointment?" Javier asked.

"It's on Friday?" I told him.

"Damn, that's in two days," Javier stated.

The three of us sat for the next forty-five minutes trying to come up with a plan We finally had something set in stone just before I left my phone rang, and it was Trevor. I put the phone on speaker so they could hear that he was still alive.

"Jessica, where the hell are you at? I know damn well it doesn't take that long to make an appointment for an abortion," Trevor said into the phone as soon as I picked up.

"Trevor, you worry too much. I'm on my way back now. I went and made the appointment then I went to the grocery store to grab some groceries."

"Did you get any steak because that's what I gotta taste for tonight? Steak and potatoes sound like a plan for dinner."

"I didn't get any steak, but I can stop at another market grab some. I should be home in about half and hour toforty-five minutes.

"Alright, I'll see you when you get here, and, Jessica, again, I'm sorry for the way I beat you last night. I should have never put my hands on you, especially while you were pregnant. Even if you're not having the baby."

"Trevor, I told you that I forgave you. I don't wanna talk about that again. And we shouldn't be talking on the phone this long, especially not about you beating on me. You're supposed to be laying low."

"You're right, that was stupid of me. I don't know what I would do to deserve a woman like you. I love you, Jessica," Trevor said.

I was caught off guard because this was the first time Trevor had told me that he loved me.

"I love you too, Trevor. I'll see you soon."

After finalizing the plan with Javier and Andrea, I got a new car and ran to the supermarket before heading back to our hideout spot.

When I got home, Trevor was sleep, so I decided to just go ahead and start dinner early. I made steak, potatoes, and asparagus. I even decided to bake a cake. I was craving all types of things, and a part of me was feeling a little excited because Trevor would no longer be a problem for me after Friday. I knew Javier was gonna kill Trevor. He was the man that killed his mother, so this was personal, and I didn't blame him. I just hoped that I could deal with the guilt of being the cause of my child's father's death.

Trevor had finally woke up from his sleep. Dinner was already prepared.

"Damn, baby. I didn't even hear you come in. You got it smelling good in here. You're not trying to poison me, are you?" Trevor joked.

"Of course, not, silly. Now come to sit down; it's time to eat.

Me and Trevor sat and had dinner like nothing ever happened. He wanted to have sex, but I couldn't do that because I was still in so much pain. But he did eat the box like it was his last meal, and I was happy about that because I knew it would be a long time before I had any sexual pleasures outside of pleasing myself.

Chapter Twenty-Four

Javier

I couldn't believe that bitch ass nigga Trevor was still alive. He was the reason why I was in a coma and almost died. Not to mention he was the one who killed my mother. Today was the day that bastard was going to die. I'd just pulled up to my parents' place to go over the final plans with my pops and a few other guys. I didn't want my father to be involved, but he insisted, and I couldn't stop him. I mean, this was the man who murdered his wife. Although I wasn't in the street life anymore, obviously, I still had connections. This was still a family business that I just chose to let someone else I trusted to run it. My wife wasn't too happy about what I was about to do, but she knew that it needed to be done. I had to protect her and my daughter no matter what. Because I didn't trust anything or anyone. I called my lawyer and made sure that everything was left to Andrea and my baby girl. I set up a trust fund for Blessing and put Andrea's name on all my houses and properties. My wife and daughter would never have to worry about money as long as they lived. Blessing would have money to raise her kids and her grandkids.

Jessica shot me a text, letting me know that she had just left the house. She told me where the key would be at and what door to use.

The house was in the damn boondocks somewhere, but that was perfect. I parked where Jessica told me to park. I also had my guys that would be the cleanup when I was finished. I didn't plan to do much talking to this nigga, but I did have a few words for him. I wanted to be in and out so I could get back home to my wife and daughter. When I walked up to the door, I heard the TV on, so I knew he was awake. I used the key to open the door, and walked in with my father and the rest of the guys behind me. I knew I didn't need all of them, but I just needed to be sure. The closer we got that to the room, I could hear that he was watching porn. He was so into beating his dick that he didn't even hear us come in. I tiptoed over to where he was sitting and put the gun to the back of his head while everyone else pointed their guns to his face.

"Go ahead and finish your nut because it's the last one you'll ever have."

"That bitch set me up?" he mumbled.

"Nah, you set yourself up the moment you came for me and my wife and killed my mother. Yeah, I get it, I killed your brother, but he was a street dude and he crossed me, so he had to be dealt with. But fuck all that. This ain't the *Orpah Show,* and I didn't come here talk—"

Before I could finish my sentence, my dad let off a round of shots in that nigga's body. And even though I knew he was dead, I shot that nigga twice in the head. I was grateful for silencers. I took a picture of his body before the cleanup crew got rid of his ass once and for all. I just wanted to give my wife and Jessica a piece of mind.

Although I still didn't fully trust Jessica, I did somewhat feel sorry for her. I thought it was crazy how much my life had changed in just a few short months. I went from being a single man running one of the largest drug empires in the world to be a married man with a daughter. I owned a club and two casinos. But in those short few months, I'd been through hell. I found out I was fucking with a cop, but I was too in love to leave her and now where married.

Once we left the house, I made sure my pops was good before heading home to my wife and daughter. I was missing them like crazy. As soon as Andrea's six weeks were up, I was having a doctor come out to make sure that she was good, then I was taking her on a surprise honeymoon. Ms. Claire agreed to come with us so she could help with the baby.

I pulled up to the house and Andrea was in the family room with Jessica pacing back and forth. As soon as Andrea saw my face, she jumped in my arms, damn near knocking me over. I was happy to see my wife too but, she's put on a couple of extra pounds after having my daughter, so she gotta chill on a nigga. I just got out of a coma.

"Oh my God, Javier, I'm so glad you're alive. I've never been so happy to see anyone in my life." Andrea started placing kisses all over my lips.

"I'm happy to see you too, baby, but I told you that I was coming back home to you and my baby girl. But, baby, you know you kinda thick, and I just got out of a coma, right?" I said, jokingly.

"Oh my God, baby, I'm sorry, but don't be talking about my thickness. You know you love it," she said, playfully punching my arm.

"You are damn right I love it," I told her kissing her soft lips.

"So, is he dead?" Jessica asked. I damn near forgot she was here.

"Hell, yeah he's dead," I assured her.

I pulled out my cell and showed her and Andrea the picture I took. Jessica gasped in horror, and Andrea just shook her head. I knew this had to be kinda hard on both the woman since they once upon of time had a relationship with his sorry ass. But I'm sure Jessica was hurting even more, especially since she was currently carrying his child when she had to be a single mother. Hopefully, she'd find a good man that would help take care of her and the baby. I told Jessica she could stay in one of the properties until she found something of her own.

I left the ladies in the living room while I went and took my shower. After I got out of the shower and got dressed, I wanted to cuddle with my baby. I walked into her nursery and she was sleeping peacefully. I picked her up, placed her in my arms, and sat in the rocking chair. She was sleeping so hard that she didn't even move when I picked her up. I gently placed a kiss on her forehead and started to sing a lullaby. I never knew it was even possible to love someone until my Blessing entered this world.

Chapter Twenty-Five

Shyanne

I walked into my shop not giving a fuck about how looked. Their asses were lucky that I even came in. My receptionist looked up at me like I was crazy. I didn't give a damn. I just came to do the two heads that I had to do, and then I was out.

"Boss, are you okay?" my receptionist, Kira, asked me.

"Kira, why the hell wouldn't I be ok? I would be even better if you stopped questioning me," I snapped.

"You don't have to speak to me that way. I was just concerned."

"I don't pay you for being concerned. I pay you to do your job, but if you keep fucking with me, you won't have one!" I yelled.

She just rolled her eyes, but she knew not to say anything else to me. Kira had been with me since day one, but she was getting on my nerves this morning. I walked into my office and place my things down. Then, I went back out front because my client should be walking in the door, but if her ass wasn't on time, she would have to reschedule. My client walked in and gave me the same look that Kira gave me, but I just rolled my eyes. This was my damn shop, and if I wanted to wear my pajamas and not unwrap my hair, that was my business.

"Hey, Shyanne. You good?"

"Why the hell is everyone worried about how I look today? You know what? Everybody get the hell out! I'm closed for the day—I'm closed until further notice!" I said, walking to the back to get my shit and bounce.

I grabbed my belongings and headed back home. When I got home, Kye was playing with the twins, and I rolled my eyes. I was over this family shit. He looked up at me and did a double-take. Kye was still asleep when I left, so he didn't see me leave.

"Baby, where are you coming from looking like that? I thought you had clients this morning?"

"If you must know, Kye, I just left my shop, and I did have clients until they got on my nerves the same way you're about to," I snapped, trying to brush past him, but he stopped me.

"You better watch how the hell you talk to me, and what the hell would make you get up and go to work like that?"

"Kye, please don't start with me. I just want to lay down," I told him.

"Wait, have you been drinking this early in the morning?"

"Kye, please just let me lay down. I didn't sign up for twenty-one questions," I told him, trying to walk by again.

But he grabbed my arm and smelled my breath. I knew I was never going to hear the end of this. "Shyanne, I cannot believe that you have been drinking this early, and now you're missing work. You have a problem, and you need to get help."

"First off, I don't have a problem. So what I had a drink before I left this morning to help me get through today. What's the problem with that?"

"The fucking problem is, it's only 9:30 in the morning. What is that you needed help getting through?"

I knew Kye was right. I'd been drinking ever since my mom died. I wasn't handling her death well, so I drank to help take my mind off of it. My dad was trying to grieve himself, and Javier had a wife and newborn of his own. Plus, he was grieving himself. Kye seemed to always be working, and when he wasn't at work, all he did was tend to the twins. I loved that he was a great father, but he forgot to be a boyfriend. I loved my kids, but for some odd reason, I didn't feel that strong motherly connection like I should've. When I watched Kye with the twins, and Javier and Andrea with my niece, they always looked so connected and loving. I just felt like I was doing a babysitting job.

"Look, Kye, maybe if you paid more attention to me instead of always working, then you'd understand. And when you not at work, all you do is play with those twins," I blurted.

"So, now it's my fault that you've turned into an alcoholic? And did you just call our kids 'those twins'? I know you're drunk, but they say a drunken mind speaks a sober tongue, and I suggest that you tread carefully."

I wasn't sure why his statement bothered me so much, but it did.

"Dread carefully or what, Kye?" I said, mushing him in the face.

I knew I shouldn't have put my hands on him, but I couldn't help it. Maybe I needed to sleep off this liquor because I was tripping. I had been drinking since last night.

"I'm telling you right now, Shyanne Santos, if you ever put your hands on me again, I'm going to stretch your ass out, and I'm not playing. You better go sleep that liquor off, and I don't want you caring for my kids while you're drinking. As a matter of a fact, we're leaving out for the day. Go sleep that shit off," Kye warned.

I might've been drunk, but I wasn't crazy. I knew not to play with Kye any further. I just walked by him, walked into my room, and slammed the door. I needed some sleep. My head was pounding.

*****

I woke up a few hours later, and my head was still pounding. It was hurting so bad that I couldn't even get up to get any pain killers. I finally dragged myself out of bed and made it the medicine cabinet. After popping four pain killers, I walked downstairs, and Kye and the kids were still not home. I was glad because I could use the peace. I walked into the kitchen to find something to eat because I was starving. For the first time, I wished I had a personal chef because I didn't feel like cooking. So I decided to order out. I walked over to the bar and poured myself a drink while I waited for my food. A half hour and two drinks later, my food still wasn't here. I heard the door, and in walked Kye and the twins. He saw the drink in my hand and looked at me with so much disgust. I never thought I'd see the day that Kye would ever look at me like that.

"I take the kids and leave for a few hours so you could get yourself together, and I get back and you're still drinking. Not to mention, I don't smell anything cooking," he stated angrily.

I just turned the glass up to my mouth and finished drinking what was in my glass, carelessly rolling my eyes. Kye mumbled something under his breath, and I let out a small chuckle. I guess I must have pissed him off because he picked up a vase and threw it on the floor. It scared the shit out of me. I had never seen Kye this angry before. He snatched the twins up and walked out the door. I just shook my head and poured another drink. I wished they hurried the hell up with my food because I was starving.

*****

It'd been a few days, and Kye and the twins still weren't home. I was starting to miss my man and my kids. I picked up the phone and dialed Kye's number, but he didn't answer. I tried calling him once more, but nothing. After I showered and got dressed, I got in the car so I could stop pass my shop. When I got there, no one was here. I looked around my place and decided that I didn't want to do hair anymore—at least not right now. I wrote a closed until further notice note and taped it to the door. I decided to go see my dad since I hadn't talked to him in over a week.

When I pulled up, I saw Kye's cars parked in front of his parent's. So I made a mental note to go pass there when I left from over here so I could see the twins. My parents and Kye's parents' houses were practically next door. When I walked inside, I was surprised to see everyone over here looking like they were having a meeting. And if that was the case, why the hell wasn't I invited?

"Hey, everyone. What's going on? Why is everyone over here?" I asked.

"Hey, Shyanne. I wasn't expecting you, but I'm glad you're here. Have a seat," my dad said.

"What's this about?"

"It's about you, sis. Kye told us about all the drinking that you've been doing and how you haven't been going to work. What's going on with you? Why are you drinking so much?" Javier asked.

"So, let me get this straight. I have a few drinks and take some days off from my fucking shop, and you come running to my family? What kinda man are you? You know what? Fuck you, Kye!" I yelled angrily.

"Shyanne, you need to watch your mouth and be glad that he cares enough about you to even say anything to your family. You need to stop talking to him like that.

Disrespecting your man is the easiest way to lose your man," my dad said sternly.

"After this stunt that he pulled, I don't even know if I want to be with his bitch ass," I let slip.

I knew that I was doing the most, and Kye didn't deserve any of my crap, but I felt like I couldn't control myself.

"I've had it with you, Shyanne. So you know what? Let me help you out. I'm done with your ass, and I'm taking my kids until you get yourself some help," Kye stated before walking out the door.

I knew I had fucked up for real.

After Kye walked out, my family went off on me. Had I known this shit was about to happen, I would have kept my ass at home. All this talk about me checking into Alcoholics Anonymous only made me want to drink even more. I hated that I was putting my family through this, but I was going through something myself. I was worse off than they knew about. If they knew how much I drank, they would just have me admitted instead of giving me an option. Tired of listening to them talk, I got up and walked out of the house. I knew I was being disrespectful, but they were stressing me out, and I really could use a drink. I didn't feel like going home and chance running into Kye, so I went to a local bar not too far from my dad's. I only planned to have one drink, but before I knew it, I was on my third glass.

"Ma'am, it's pretty early, and you're already waisted. Maybe you should call someone to come pick you up."

"I'm a grown ass woman. You don't tell me when I've had too much to drink. Now pour me another round," I told the bartender in a drunken slur.

"I'm afraid I'm gonna have to cut you off."

"Give me another damn drink before I burn this bitch down!" I yelled.

The bartender just looked at me and walked to the back. When he came back to the front, he wouldn't say anything to me, no matter what I said to him. He also wouldn't give me anything else to drink. A few minutes later, my dad and Javier walked in the bar, and I immediately got pissed and started acting a fool.

"I don't know what the hell you called them for because I'm not going anywhere with them!"

"Shyanne, get your ass up and let's go. You ought to be a shamed of yourself for acting a drunken fool this early in the morning. This is an embarrassment to the entire family!" my dad yelled.

I just rolled my eyes.

"Shy, let's go before I drag your ass out of here. I have shit to do today and don't have time to fuck around with you all day," Javier said.

"Fuck you, Javier! You're you're not the boss of me, and I didn't ask you to come down here anyway! Now leave me alone!"

I guess Javier had just about enough of my shit, so he walked over and picked me up and threw me over his shoulders like I was a little ass kid. He opened my car door and put me in the backseat. I swear it felt like the car was spinning. Javier pulled up in front of his house, and now I was really confused as to why I was here. I wanted to go home. Not be here with him and his perfect little family.

"Take me home!" I yelled while kicking and screaming like a small ass child, but he didn't pay my ass any mind.

Javier took me down to the space that Andrea was locked up at and left me down there. I wasn't having it at first, but eventually, I passed out on the bed.

Chapter Twenty-Six

Andrea

"Good morning, mommy's little princess. Are you ready to see daddy's surprise? I know I'm ready," I cooed to Blessing.

Javier said that he had a big surprise for Blessing and myself, and I couldn't wait to see what it was. I wasn't sure how much you could surprise an almost two-month-old, but I didn't put anything past Javier. Blessing just smiled at me like she knew what I was talking about. Waking up to her pretty face every morning was a blessing itself. Blessing was a beautiful baby. She had features of me and Javier, but she had my complexion, and you could tell that she was mixed.

"Hey, baby. Are you about ready?" Javier said, walking up behind me and placing a kiss on my neck.

"Yes, baby. I'm ready. Just give me a small hint on what the surprise is."

"Nope. Then it wouldn't be a surprise. Now give me my daughter and hurry up," he said, taking Blessing out of my arms.

Blessing was Javier's world. The way she acted when he entered the room or picked her up, I knew she was going to be a daddy's girl. He went and tatted her entire name and birthday on his arm, along with her baby picture. Javier was already talking about having another baby, but that was the last thing on my mind. I loved Blessing with everything in me, but I wasn't even sure if I wanted any more kids, especially if I have to endure that kind of pain again.

I just had my six-week checkup, and the doctor gave me the green light to have sex a few days ago, yet, suddenly, Javier wanted to wait a few extra days. On the other hand, I was horny as hell. I was getting some dick before the day was over. Even if I had to take it.

When I got downstairs, Javier was putting the baby in the car. I was surprised to see that Ms. Claire was going with us. I decided not to ask any more questions. I just rolled with it and waited to be surprised. About a half hour later, we were pulling up to an airport. Now I was really curious about where we were going.

"Oh my God, Javier, why are we at the airport, and where are we going?" I asked excitedly.

"Chill. You'll find out shortly," he told me with a big ass smile.

The three of us got out the car and walked into the airport. He stopped at the customer service desk for a brief moment before we walked outside. I haven't flown much, but this didn't look like the standard procedure. We walked outside, and it was a guy, that I take was a pilot, standing up against a plane that read *Javier's*. I just knew that Javier didn't have his own airplane, but I was wrong. He owned his own plane. We all boarded, and I had to admit it was nice as hell on the inside.

"Oh my God, Javier. This is nice. I didn't even know you owned a private plane."

"*We* own a lot of things that you don't know about. You have to stop saying *I*, Andrea. It's *we*. Then, once we leave this earth, everything will go to our children."

I leaned over and kissed Javier on the lips. I truly loved this man, and to think that I almost gave all of this up. I thought back to when Javier had me hostage right in his place. I thought he had me in an upscale warehouse, but I was right at his house the entire time. I was just in the basement, but that basement was like an apartment. I had a glass of wine and something light to eat while we flew. I was a little nervous flying with Blessing at such a young age, but I said a silent prayer for God to protect us all.

Almost four hours later, the plane had finally landed at our destination. I still had no idea why we didn't pack anything if we were catching a flight. Javier finished up with feeding Blessing before deboarded. To my surprise, there was a car waiting for us when we got off. As we were driving, I noticed a sign that said welcome to Jamaica.

"Oh my God, we're in Jamaica? This was my mother's hometown!" I said in excitement.

"That's right, baby, we're in Jamaica," Javier said with a big smile.

About twenty minutes later, we pulled up to a giant house. Whose house? I wasn't sure, but the outside was beautiful. When we got to the door, we were greeted with a woman and a man holding a tray of drinks.

"Good afternoon, Mr. and Mrs. Santos," the man and the woman said in unison.

Both of us spoke back and proceeded into the house. As I walked, I damn near lost my breath. That' how beautiful it was. It was housekeepers and servants throughout the house. They gave us a tour, and the more rooms I saw, the more in love I fell with the dwelling. We were still downstairs. We walked out to the yard, and it was just as beautiful outside as it was inside. And the pool was everything you could dream of. It was finally time to go back to the main level. I thought we were going to take the stairs like normal people, but nope. We took an elevator. All six of seven of the rooms that I saw, including the nursery, were beautiful.

"Thanks for the tour. I have it from here," Javier said to the tourist.

He then walked me over to another elevator. When we got on, he pushed the third floor. When we got off the elevator, it was just one room sitting by itself.

"Go ahead, baby. Open the door."

I turned the handles to open the door, and when I walked in the room, I threw my hands over my face in disbelief. The room was huge with a big ass banner across the bed that said *Welcome to Your Honeymoon*. After everything that we'd been through, he still managed to take me on a honeymoon. I loved Javier so much. I was so proud to be Mrs. Santo.

"Oh my God, Javier, this is beautiful! I love you so much!" I told him.

This room made me even hornier than I already was. Wasting no time, I started taking Javier's clothes off.

"Damn, I see somebody is ready." Javier chuckled.

"You are damn right I'm ready. You about to get the business," I told him, biting down on my bottom lip.

Javier loved when I bit down on my lip. He said it was sexy as hell, and that it was a big turn on for him.

"Oh, is that right?" he asked.

I climbed on top of Javier and placed kisses all over his body. He groaned and all that did was turn me on even more. As soon as I got to his thickness, I placed it in my wet, warm mouth and gently sucked it until it swelled up. I made sure to gag on it just the way he liked it.

"Fuck, Drea," he moaned while biting his lip.

I loved to suck his manhood while seductively looking him in his eyes. For the next hour, Javier and I explored one another's bodies, making eachother cum more time than we could count. I was way overdue for some dick, and apparently, he was overdue for some of me too. I was nice and ready for a nap. Between the flight and our sex session, I was worn out.

*****

Later that night, the four of us went swimming. Blessing was loving the water, and Ms. Claire was enjoying herself as well. I still couldn't believe how beautiful this place was.

"Baby, how long did you rent this place for? It's beautiful. I love it here," I told him honestly.

"Yes, this is beautiful. I've never really done much traveling, but I could get used to this," Ms. Claire chimed in.

"Well, I'm glad you like it, and to answer your question, this is our vacation home. So we can stay for as long as you want, baby. This is a much-needed vacation, and you deserve the world, Andrea."

"Oh my God, Javier, are you serious?"

"I'm serious as a heart attack," he answered.

"Wow. What did I do to deserve you? If we weren't already married, I would marry you again."

"The question is, what did I do to deserve you? Andrea, you and my daughter made me a better man, and I'll love you for the rest of my life," Javier stated, looking me dead in the eyes.

I swear if Blessing and Ms. Claire wasn't in this pool, I would have been making love to him right now.

"I think me, and little Miss Blessing should give you two newlyweds some alone time," Ms. Claire said with a big smile.

"Thank you, Ms. Claire," Javier said.

Me, myself, was embarrassed that we were behaving like that in front of her. Although Ms. Claire was cool as shit. I loved me some Ms. Claire. I wondered if she ever got lonely because I never saw her go anywhere or have a company. She was a beautiful woman with extremely long her and had a nice ass body for her age. As soon as Ms. Claire and Blessing went into the house, my husband didn't waste any time taking off my bathing suit and slow stroking me right there in the pool. Javier brought me to just pure ecstasy.

Chapter Twenty-Seven

Javier

We'd just got back to the states after being gone for a little over three weeks. I truly enjoyed myself and was glad that my wife, as well as, Ms. Claire, had fun. I had a couple more surprises for my wife and Ms. Claire. We'd just left the airport and was on our way to one of my surprises. We finally were at our destination, and I could already tell that my wife was confused.

"Javier, where are we going now? Wherever it is, it's beautiful," she said.

"Just follow me." We all got out of the car and walked into the house

"Oh, this house is beyond beautiful," Ms. Claire said to herself.

"Yes, it is, but whose house is it?" Andrea asked.

I didn't bother to answer her. I just handed her an envelope. She took the envelope and opened it up. I watched her eyes scan the paper, then they got so wide that I thought they were gonna pop out of her head. She starting jumping up and down like a small child.

"Oh my God, Javier, this is just too much!"

"Well, I want to know what's going on," Ms. Claire joked.

"This is our new home. I've been having this house built for some time. I found one of Andrea's sketchbooks, and she had a house that looked just like this one. It was labeled my dream house. So, I figured why not have her dream house made."

The look on Andrea's face was priceless. I could see the tears forming in her eyes. "Javier, you're a great man. This was sweet of you. I didn't even know you saw my sketches. Those were something that I use to do when I was a little girl, but this right here is beyond amazing. I can't even get my thoughts together. I'm speechless, Javier, but thank you so much. I will never be able to match what you do for me," Andrea stated with so much sincerity in her voice.

"Andrea, you already match me. You've out done me. These are material things, Andrea. What you do to me is deep within, and that's something that could never be matched. Not to mention you gave me my daughter. Just for that, you deserve this and so much more."

"Javier, why does this deed only have my name listed?" she quizzed.

"Because this is your house. No matter what, this will always be yours unless you decide to sell it, but it will be yours to sell. I have one more surprise, and then I'm done."

Andrea looked at me like I was crazy, but this surprise was for the other special one in my life.

"Ms. Claire, you have been around since before I was born. You're a second mother to me. Hell, with all due respect, at times, you were more like my first mother. I say all of that to say this. For as long as I could remember, you were always with us. and I never saw you with a man. You rarely go out, and you never had any children of your own. Me and Shyanne were the only kids that you had. Well, I think it's time for you to live your life and spend all that money that you have saved up. I also brought you a house and got you a personal chef, as well as a maid. You deserve the world, and you can't have that working for me for the rest of your life. You're more than welcome here anytime you like. Your place isn't too far from here," I told her.

Ms. Claire just cried, and when I say she cried? I mean, she cried. She walked over and held me tight for what seemed like forever. Hell, she made me get teary-eyed.

"Javier. all I can say is, this comes as a complete shock to me, and I love you more than you could ever imagine.

You're the son I never had, and I can't say thank you enough," Ms. Claire cried.

"You're welcome Momma C. Now let's get you to your new place," I told her.

We headed to the car and rode to her place.

*****

It'd been two weeks since we got back from the islands, and things were just starting to get back to normal from all the excitement. Now I was about to go and chill. Kye, my man, needed someone to talk to since my sister was putting him through hell. Shyanne was hell, and she was taking this drinking shit to far. Shit was so bad, Kye took the twins and moved out.

I pulled up to Kye's new place, and just the outside alone was nice. But Kye had always had good taste, so I wasn't surprised. When I walked in, Kye was playing *Madden*. He paused the game when he noticed me and gave me some dap.

"Damn, bro. It seems like I haven't seen your ass in a month of Sundays. Wassup with you? I'm loving the new spot," I told Kye.

"Shit, just been chilling and taking care of my kids. The highlight of my life. Your sister is still fucking up and refuses to get any help. That shit is hurting a nigga's heart watching her ruin her life like that. We have two beautiful kids, and she's missing out on their most precious moments. I take them over to see her whenever her ass is sober. I almost killed her ass a couple of weeks ago. I walked in and she was fucking some nigga."

My eyes got wide as hell because I would have killed her ass too. The thought of Andrea fucking another nigga made my skin crawl. I would've been and killed both of their asses.

"Damn, Kye. This shit is crazy, but I'm going to stop by there when I leave here, and I'm putting her ass in a program today because this is unacceptable," I told him seriously.

We kicked it for a little, but I didn't stay too much later because I was serious about putting Shyanne's ass in a program, rather she likes it or not. As soon as I left Kye's, I called a few places, but it was one particular that I was interested in. I explained the situation and told them we would be there shortly. I got to Shyanne's in about twenty minutes. I didn't even bother to knock. I used my key and walked in. I couldn't believe the way this house looked. My sister never kept a dirty house. I walked to her bedroom, and she was laid up with some nigga. I woke that nigga up from his sleep.

"Yo', get the fuck up and get the fuck out, now!" I yelled.

"Nigga, who the fuck are you?"

"Who I am ain't important. Just get the fuck out before I beat our ass," I warned. I was in the mood to play no games with this nigga.

"Javier, what the hell are you doing? Why are you kicking him out? This is my house," Shyanne's drunk ass said, pissing me off.

"Shyanne, shut your drunk ass up and put some clothes on. You have five minutes, or I'm coming to drag you out this room."

The punk ass nigga she was laid up with got his shit and rolled out. A few minutes later, Shyanne came out looking half-decent with a smug look on her face.

"Let's go, Shyanne. We have somewhere to be," I told her.

"Nigga, I'm not going anywhere. I'm tired. I was up all night," she whined.

I didn't say shit else to her. I picked her little ass up and threw her over my shoulder before walking to my car.

When I got the car, I put the childproof locks on and drove to my destination. Of course, she was performing and yelling for me to take her back home, but I wasn't paying her ass any mind. An hour and a half, later we pulled up to the program. I got out of the car and opened the door. Her little ass was strong as hell. She was swinging, but I didn't care because her ass was going to check into this program.

I finally got her in the building, and once she realized how serious this was, she started crying. That's when I started to feel bad for her. I hated to see my sister like this, but she needed help, and she needed it fast. She had two babies to raise. I knew that one of the main reasons she was drinking was because my mom died and she couldn't handle it. And I'm sure trying to take care of two babies at once, while tring to grieve the death of your mom, was a lot to deal with.

"Javier, please don't leave me here. I swear I'm going to stop drinking. Just please don't leave me here, bro, please?" Shyanne cried.

This shit was breaking my heart, but I had to do it. I signed the paperwork, wrote a check, and left out. I could still hear Shyanne screaming and crying from the car. Leaving my sister against her will was one of the hardest things I ever had to do.

Epilogue
One year later

Jessica

"Honey, where you at?" my husband, Johnathan, yelled.

"I'm in the kitchen."

Jonathan walked in and kissed the back of my neck. We'd been married for three months, but we'd been together for nine. Not too long after Trevor was killed, I moved to New York. It just wasn't anything left for me in Jersey but bad memories. Jonathan used to be my neighbor. Once we started talking, we hit it off immediately. I was just three months, pregnant and now, my son Demarcus was almost a year old. My son and husband were the best things that had ever happened to me. I loved my new life. I wasn't a cop any more. I currently wasn't working. I had enough money to live a good life, not to mention I was getting all of Trevor's benefits since my son was the only child.

I still kept in touch with Andrea. She and Javier were just here a few weeks ago. It was great seeing them. I was a stay at home mom and for fun, I started writing a book. I didn't plan to publish, but I did want to write. Well, that's about it for me. I have my son and my husband, and that was good enough for me.

Ms. Claire

Ever since Javier took me to Jamaica and brought me a house, I have been living my best life. I got myself a husband and all we did was travel the world and have great sex. I was fifty years old and couldn't have been happier. I know what y'all thinking. How the hell did I find a man and get married so quickly? Well, I've known my husband for years, and once we started hanging out, we couldn't fight the chemistry. So we decided to be with one another, and we're both too old to be dating for years when we already knew what we wanted. I was proud to be Mrs. Santos. You heard right, I married Franklin Santos. I went from working for him to working him as much as I could in a day.

At first, we didn't know how Javier and Shyanne would feel about us being together and their father remarrying so soon. But to our surprise, they were good with it. They were happy for us. So that made things a lot easier. We moved into my place because Franklin didn't want to disrespect his late wife. I completely understood. Well, it was nice while it lasted. I have to go. I have a husband to tend to.

Shyanne

After my mom was killed at my brother's wedding, that shit took a serious toll on me. Not to mention, my brother was in a coma, and then right after that, I had a set of twins with no time to grieve. So, yes, I started drinking, and that shit got out of hand. The day Javier forced me to go to a program, I hated him and swore I would never speak to him again. But once I was clean and back to myself, I had no choice but to respect and love him even more for loving me enough to make me get better for the sake of kids. Speaking of my kids, they were a year and a half and getting into everything. I opened up two more salons, but I stopped doing hair. The only head I did was Andrea's. I decided to be a stay at home mom.

I had missed enough time away from them, and I wanted to spend every moment I could with them. As far as me and Kye, I had fucked that up big time, and he wasn't fucking with me for a minute. He was even fucking around with some bitch for a little bit, but I wasn't having that. Now, even though we're taking things one day at a time, we were back together, and I was happy about that. Kye was the love of my life and I almost lost him completely. I'm not proud of the person that I was, but I'm damn sure glad that it made me become the woman I was today. Me and Andrea were close as thieves. She was truly the sister that I never had. I could see why Javier was so in love with her. Well, that's it for me. Life was good with me now that I finally got my shit together, thanks to my brother.

Andrea

"Javier are you ready to go yet? You know this is a big night for me, and now we're going to be running late because you wanted some before we left. This is the reason why I'm in the predicament I'm in now because you always want to be nasty."

"Yes, I'm ready, and you know you love every bit of my nasty ass. Hell, you're probably nastier than me," Javier stated while walking down the stairs. "And you're pregnant because you starting forgetting to take your birth control. You probably did it on purpose so you could trap me into wanting to be with you. I mean, look at how fine I am, and how much money I have," he joked. My husband did the most. He was such a play fiend.

"Nigga, please. I'm pregnant because you can't get enough of this WAP."

Javier just busted out laughing.

After he reminded me of a hobby I used to love, I started doing sketches, and now I owned my art gallery. I was making so much money from my drawings, and I was just drawing for fun. I talked all that shit about not having another baby, and here I was pregnant with my second child a year later. I was kind of excited, especially since we found out a couple of days ago that we were having a boy.

Now our family would be complete. We were still debating on a name, but we'd figure it out. We still had a little way to go.

Javier also now owned a chain of casinos and his club. He did a lot of his work from home because he hated to be away from me and Blessing for too long. I was amazed at how life turned out for me. I went from being an officer of the law to marrying a kingpin, then having my boss killed, and having a baby.

Yup, I was in love, and it felt so good to be loved the way Javier loved me. My daughter was my world, and I couldn't wait to have my son. I was officially in love with the wrong side of the law.

The End.

Are you in search of a good publishing home?
Tyanna Presents just may be the perfect place for you!

We are currently accepting submissions in the
following genres:

URBAN FICTION
URBAN ROMANCE
WOMEN'S FICTION
STREET LIT
BWWM
PARANORMAL
EROTICA
SUSPENSE

For consideration, please submit the first 3 chapters
of your manuscript to:

TYANNAPRESENTS1@GMAIL.COM